COVERT AMISH
INVESTIGATION

DANA R. LYNN

LOVE INSPIRED SUSPENSE
INSPIRATIONAL ROMANCE

LOVE INSPIRED® SUSPENSE
INSPIRATIONAL ROMANCE

Recycling programs
for this product may
not exist in your area.

ISBN-13: 978-1-335-55457-4

Covert Amish Investigation

Copyright © 2021 by Dana Roae

This edition published by arrangement with Harlequin Books S.A.

For questions and comments about the quality of this book, please contact us at CustomerService@Harlequin.com.

Love Inspired
22 Adelaide St. West, 40th Floor
Toronto, Ontario M5H 4E3, Canada
www.Harlequin.com

Printed in U.S.A.

9.5

"I feel like I'm being watched."

Abram's face hardened. Kate knew he was planning on going after whoever it was. Without thinking, she grabbed his arm, letting the basket slide to the ground.

His gaze shot to her hand holding his arm, then back to her face.

"Think, Abram. He probably has a knife or a gun, if anyone's there. What would you do?"

"I would give you time to escape."

Her mouth fell open and she gaped at him. He'd risk his life so she could escape. Had he always been so noble?

"Abram, I'm the one with a gun hidden in my apron."

His face froze. "You have a gun?"

"I'm a cop, remember?"

She saw the glint of sunlight striking steel.

"Get down!"

A gunshot cracked through the quiet. The taut clothesline snapped as the bullet ripped through it.

She never knew how it happened. One moment they were standing side by side, and the next Abram had pushed her down and was protecting her with his own body.

Dana R. Lynn grew up in Illinois. She met her husband at a wedding and told her parents she'd met the man she was going to marry. Nineteen months later, they were married. Today, they live in rural Pennsylvania with their three children and a variety of animals. In addition to writing, she works as a teacher for the deaf and hard of hearing and is active in her church.

Books by Dana R. Lynn

Love Inspired Suspense

Amish Country Justice

Plain Target
Plain Retribution
Amish Christmas Abduction
Amish Country Ambush
Amish Christmas Emergency
Guarding the Amish Midwife
Hidden in Amish Country
Plain Refuge
Deadly Amish Reunion
Amish Country Threats
Covert Amish Investigation

Visit the Author Profile page at Harlequin.com.

For I know the thoughts that I think toward you, saith the Lord, thoughts of peace, and not of evil, to give you an expected end.
—*Jeremiah* 29:11

To my editor, Tina James,
and to my agent, Tamela Hancock Murray.
I appreciate having you in my corner
more than I can say. Thank you!

ONE

"**Y**ou want me to go where?" Officer Kate Bontrager blurted. She winced at the thread of panic twisting through her words. Her stomach warped itself into a knotted ball. She prayed she'd misheard her captain. But she knew she hadn't.

Her partner, Sergeant Shane Pearson, shot her a questioning glance, but she kept her eyes glued to the woman sitting behind the desk. He had to be wondering what was going on, but she didn't enlighten him. She liked Shane. He and his wife, Marnie, were like family. There were parts of her past, however, that she had never told anyone.

"You heard me." Captain Sarah Murphy's mouth straightened into a thin line. "You know I wouldn't ask you to return to Sutter Springs unless it was important."

The captain pushed a black-and-white picture across the wooden surface toward her officers. A young woman in her midtwenties stared back at them, her pretty face surrounded by a bonnet. She was wearing a simple unadorned dress. A typical Amish woman from the tiny community in Berlin County, Ohio.

Except this wasn't an Amish woman.

"That's Bailey St. Andrews!" As soon as the words rushed from Kate's mouth, Shane frowned, confused. She shrugged. "Sorry. I was part of the team that responded to the 911 call when her ex-boyfriend tried to kill her."

Bailey had been a wealthy socialite and the heiress to her father's estate, which was worth millions. Her face had been plastered across magazines and young girls everywhere had longed to be in her shoes. All that counted for nothing when she had entered into an abusive relationship.

Her captain nodded. "Yes, and that's why I need you, Kate. Bailey St. Andrews was placed in witness protection three years ago. Her testimony was crucial in shutting down a major crime ring and putting many of the players involved behind bars. Including her ex-boyfriend, Vincent Mayfield. Because of the scope of the crime ring run by her ex, and her own high profile, she was sent to an Amish community in Sutter Springs. No one else knows the Amish culture like you." She leaned across the desk, her eyes boring into Kate's. "No one knows Sutter Springs like you do. It's a booming district, lots of tourist traffic. We need someone who can blend in."

The pit in her stomach yawned wide open. She wasn't going to be able to talk herself out of this. After all, she'd lived in that same Amish culture until Gary the Shark had entered her life and destroyed everything that was good and beautiful. He'd come close to destroying her, too.

The heavy feeling in Kate's gut ramped up to a full-out cramp. She kept her posture ramrod straight with difficulty. She shook herself free of the memories to focus on her captain's words.

"There's been no contact with her for the past month," the captain continued while Kate felt the walls around her sliding in closer. "When her handler went to check on her, she found that Beth Zook, Bailey's name in the community, hadn't shown up to work for a week and her house was a mess. Whether from someone searching it or from her resisting an attacker, we don't know. There has also been more crime activity in the area. Drugs, a child was almost abducted. The US Marshals think someone is using the Amish community as a front. With all the tourists through the area, it's a prime place for crime to go unnoticed."

"What about Bailey's ex-boyfriend?" Kate asked. That seemed to be the most logical question.

"Beth," the chief corrected her. "You need to get used to referring to her as Beth."

Kate nodded. It wouldn't do to slip up and reveal the woman's true identity. "Beth, then."

She waited for the captain to answer her question.

"He's still in jail." Captain Murphy folded her hands on her desk. Her gaze was direct. The barest hint of sympathy lurked in her deep brown eyes. Did she know how hard this would be for Kate? "If someone in his crime ring has decided to take over and relocate, we'd like to know about it."

"You think someone took her?"

The captain nodded. "We hope that's the case. I would much rather find out that she was an innocent than that she was involved in the crime ring this whole time."

So would she. "You said she had a job. What was it?"

"She'd been working as a housekeeper for the Amish-run bed-and-breakfast."

Well. Housekeeper was about as far removed from her former socialite lifestyle as you could get.

Sutter Springs. How much had changed since she'd been there last? When she was growing up, the tourist businesses were just getting started. *Englischers* loved to come and see how the Plain folk lived. It was lucrative for the districts that decided to take part. Kate's parents hadn't approved, but since the bishop and most of the elders were on board, there was nothing more to be said.

Her parents hadn't approved of many things. Including Kate. Nope, she wasn't going there. She turned her thoughts back to what she recalled of Sutter Springs. Right outside Berlin, there had been a steady stream of visitors yearlong. Apparently, that was still the case.

Funny. She didn't recall a bed-and-breakfast. But she'd been gone since she was sixteen. That was almost ten years ago. Did Abram still live there?

She wrenched her mind from thoughts of the boy she'd loved and left without a word.

"Kate," Captain Murphy cut in. "You're familiar with the Amish lifestyle. That means you'd be able blend in while Shane will be able to try to learn more from the non-Amish people in the area. Plus, you already know what Beth looks like. We can't exactly flash a picture of her around. The bishop wants to keep this quiet. If anyone gets wind of the fact that we were hiding her there, she could be put into more danger— assuming she wasn't involved in the first place. And that's what we're going with at the moment. Her handler will meet you in Sutter Springs to give you further information."

Kate's lungs tightened, desperate for air that seemed to have been sucked from the room. She wanted to refuse. Oh, how she wished she could say no! The idea of going back to that place was like standing on the edge of a black hole unable to avoid being sucked into it.

They spent a couple more minutes discussing their travel plans. The captain informed Kate she'd have the appropriate clothes for her disguise by the next day. Kate gave her a wooden nod. When they were dismissed, she left the office, her mind whirling in shock. She made it back to her desk on autopilot and sank into her chair.

She was really going to have go back there. What if she saw Gary the Shark? Or Abram Burkholder?

Kate squeezed her eyes shut against the image of a young man with wavy dark brown hair and eyes the color of the cappuccino she loved so much. In her memories, Abram Burkholder was always smiling or laughing. What would he say if he saw her? She swallowed. Maybe they wouldn't cross paths. If he'd married, he could have moved on to a different district.

"You okay, kid? Looking a little green there."

Her eyes swept up to find Shane hovering near her desk, his forehead creased in concern. Her first instinct was to deny it. But he was her partner. He deserved to know.

"I left that world for a reason, Shane. Something really bad happened to me, and when I lost my parents, I got out of there."

His hand clamped on her shoulder for a moment.

"Do you want me to talk with the captain, see if I can get you out of it?"

He would do it if she so much as nodded. She'd been fortunate to have an officer of his caliber take her under his wing and mentor her. He was still looking out for her, even though she was no longer a complete rookie.

For the barest millisecond, she was tempted to let him before her common sense reasserted itself. The captain had been correct. Her knowledge of the Amish and Sutter Springs would be an asset. "Thanks, Shane. I appreciate the thought, but I'm a cop. I'm not going to refuse to do an assignment to protect my feelings."

Approval gleamed from his gaze. She'd done the right thing. But doing the right thing didn't untie the knots in her stomach.

Two days later, on Wednesday, they were on their way to Sutter Springs. Kate's hands had trembled the tiniest bit when Captain Murphy handed her two Amish dresses in different shades of pink and the pristine starched prayer *kapp*. She'd also shown Kate the white apron that had been altered to allow Kate to secretly carry her weapon and cell phone. Kate had accepted the items without a word, knowing if she said anything her voice would have cracked and given her away.

She hadn't been able to convince herself to put the clothes on, though. Not yet. For now, she was dressed in jeans and a T-shirt. Her blue jean jacket had been flung across her bag in the back seat.

She stared out at the trees dotting the landscape beside the interstate. In a few weeks, the leaves would begin changing. She shivered. September thirteenth fell on a Monday this year. That was only five days away. It was the most dreaded day of the year. For her, anyway.

As they got closer to their destination, she straightened.

"Hold on, Shane. We're getting really close to where Bailey—Beth—lived. Let's stop there first and see if we can see anything. The captain gave me a key to her house."

Once they were there, she'd change into one of the dresses. Distaste tasted like ashes on her tongue.

When Shane pulled into the drive, she directed him to pull all the way behind the house.

"We'll use the back door."

Kate stepped out of the vehicle. It was a little chilly. She opened the back door and grabbed her jacket and swung it on, taking a moment to scan the area. The house was set back from the road, large trees on either side of the gravel driveway. The lawn was overgrown by a few inches. Gauging by the otherwise pristine condition of the lawn, this was not the norm. Looking up at the structure, she noted without surprise that there were no curtains in the window. As far as she could see, nothing had been disturbed in the yard.

"You coming?" Shane called out.

She nodded and followed as he headed up to the house. Shane paused at the bottom of the steps.

"Back up." He grabbed his service weapon from its holster and continued in a whisper, "The door's open a hair."

"The captain said Beth's handler had been here and seen the house was a wreck."

"Yeah, but they would have shut the door when they left."

Nodding, Kate pulled her own gun out and moved back and to the side. From where she stood, a sliver of the wooden floor on the other side of the door was visible. She could see some debris on the floor. Narrowing her eyes, she leaned forward, trying to analyze what she was seeing. It looked like a black bonnet was on the floor. The kind Amish women wore over their prayer *kapps* when they left their house. Had Beth planned on leaving or was she taken?

The bottom step creaked when Shane stepped on it. When he placed his right foot on the next stair up, the only warning was a soft click before the porch exploded, sending Shane, Kate and splintered wood flying.

"Ah, Abram. *Cumme.*"

Abram Burkholder stepped into Bishop Melvin Hershberger's *haus*, removing his hat and placing it on a peg near the door. He nodded his head respectfully to Edith Hershberger, the bishop's *frau*. She smiled in response. Color seared his ears. Linda, the woman he'd almost married, was her cousin. There was no reproach on her face, though, so she probably didn't know the story.

"*Koffee*, Abram? It's fresh and hot." She reached for a mug, her hand suspended as she waited for his response.

"*Danke, nee.*" He'd already had two cups today. One more cup and he'd never be able to sleep tonight. And he desperately needed to sleep.

The aroma of freshly baked bread and a hearty stew reminded Abram that it was nearly suppertime. Not that there was anything to hurry home for. His *mamm* would have supper ready. However, Abram worked with his father and brother in the family painting business. They'd tell her not to expect him.

And he had no wife. He'd courted Linda for six months. He'd even asked her to marry him. To his surprise, she'd turned him down flat.

You don't love me, she'd accused him. *Is there someone else you love?*

He'd denied it, of course. He would never court a woman if he were seeing someone else.

She wasn't all wrong, though. Mortified, he realized that his memories were still too full of Katie Bontrager, the girl he'd once believed he'd marry. Before she'd left without a word and broken his heart.

Abram followed the bishop into the large main room. Bishop Hershberger was a wiry man in his late thirties. He shut the door to the office and gestured for Abram to sit. Abram lowered himself into one of the sturdy wooden chairs and watched the bishop settle himself in the other chair. Abram waited for him to speak. Bishop Hershberger had asked him to stop by on his way home from his shop, so he'd hitched up his buggy and come, bone weary from the hectic day. One did not refuse the bishop's personal request.

Bishop Hershberger considered him for a few moments before speaking. "Abram, it seems we have a problem."

Abram raised his eyebrows. He didn't have a clue what the bishop was referring to. He wracked his brain, trying to think of any infractions at his shop, but none came to mind. He was very careful to abide by all the rules.

The face of Katie Bontrager swam before his eyes

before he shoved it away. She was out of his life. Her own choice, though he'd never known why. Nor was he likely to.

"Have I done something wrong?"

Bishop Hershberger waved his hand. "*Nee*. You have done nothing to be concerned about. I called you here about a more troubling matter. We have had a member disappear. Beth Zook. Are you familiar with her?"

"*Ja*, I know who she is, but I haven't talked with her much. She's a bit shy. She works at the Plain and Simple Bed and Breakfast, ain't so?" He thought back. "Or she did. My *onkel* says she hasn't shown up in a while."

His *onkel* and *aenti* ran the B&B.

The bishop nodded. "*Ja*. What you don't know, what no one knows, is that she was not raised Amish. She was placed here as part of the *Englisch* witness protection program."

Abram stared at him. "An *Englisch* woman? In witness protection here? I would have thought that was against our rules."

It was hard to wrap his mind around it. Yet, at the same time, it made sense. He'd met Beth on several occasions. While she'd said all the right things, her eyes had seemed haunted. He'd shrugged the feeling of wrongness away, but now he understood.

The bishop's troubled eyes met his. "Abram, I believe that we need to be charitable. This young woman, while not one of us, came to us for a safe haven. We granted her that. She didn't mingle much, but she was taking classes to become Amish of her own free will. I fear something horrible has happened to her."

Disturbed, Abram leaned forward. "I guess I assumed she decided to quit. What do you think might have happened?"

"I don't know. Maybe nothing. But I need your help." The older man leaned in, his deep eyes piercing. "I've contacted the *Englisch* marshal who placed her here. She contacted the police department that had been connected with Beth's case before she came to us and they're sending officers to come and investigate. They'll be staying at the bed-and-breakfast. I want you to help them. I also want you to keep an eye on them."

Abram understood. The Amish rarely involved outsiders, especially law enforcement. What he didn't understand was why he was the bishop's choice.

"Not the Sutter Springs police?"

The bishop shrugged. "Who knows the way of the *Englisch* law? The way she explained it to me, the fewer people who knew the truth about Beth, the safer she was. The Sutter Springs police are aware of the crime in the area, just not Beth's true identity."

Abram nodded and moved on to his next question.

"Why me?" That sounded too brusque. "I am always willing to help, but I don't really know this woman. I'm not sure I'm the best choice to help."

"One of the officers coming used to be Amish. It will be unsettling for the officer to return, even for a short while."

His eyebrows shot up. "A former Amish officer is going to pretend to be Amish again?"

This was getting stranger by the moment.

"*Ja*. Abram, you are young and single. You have a good head on your shoulders and are usually calm in a tough situation. It was only a few years ago that your own brother Levi returned to us. It was a difficult transition, but now look at him. He's married with two *kinder* and he's a deacon in the church. Having seen his struggle, I think you would be a *gut* support for the officer."

Restless, Abram stood and walked to the window. He struggled to wrap his mind around what the bishop said. In the distance, the sky was dark. He leaned closer to the window, then jumped back when flames shot above the trees. In the direction of his home, his business and many other Amish establishments.

"There's a fire! I need to go."

He grabbed his hat and headed to his buggy. He climbed up, aware of the bishop clambering up on the other side. Abram pressed his lips together. He wasn't going to argue with the man. If there was a fire, every able-bodied man would be welcome.

Instead, he grabbed the reins and set his mare off on a trot. Her hooves kicked up dust and gravel against the plastic shield on the front of the buggy. Once he reached the street, he halted the mare long enough to ascertain that no one was coming from either way before setting her off again.

The siren reached him first, then a short minute later, the fire truck passed him. *Gut*. Sometimes, a call went out when most of the volunteers were at work. When that happened, a *haus* would burn down before anyone arrived. Thirty seconds later, an ambulance swept by and Abram's heart thudded. Someone had been injured. He heard the bishop mutter a prayer. Abram wanted to pray, but the words were stuck. When had he last prayed spontaneously?

The fact that he couldn't remember sent shame trickling through him. He pushed it down, not wanting to be distracted. A few minutes later, they cleared the trees.

The fire truck was parked in a driveway, its red-and-white lights flashing.

It was the *haus* of the missing woman they'd been talking about ten minutes earlier.

"That's Beth's *haus*!" Bishop Hershberger echoed his thoughts.

Abram pulled the buggy to the side of the road. The bishop hopped down almost before the wheels stopped turning, startling Abram. He had never seen him move so fast. Abram jumped down and followed. The ambulance was parked beyond the *haus*. Rounding the corner of the *haus*, he gaped. The back porch had been obliterated, leaving behind a pile of smoldering debris. Scorch marks covered the back wall. The firefighters aimed the continuous rush of water at the site even though the flames appeared to be out. Abram was glad they were being cautious as sometimes fires restarted if the embers weren't taken care of.

Movement at the ambulance caught his attention. Paramedics maneuvered the stretcher carrying a man who looked a bit older than Abram into the ambulance. Burns covered his face and arms and what was left of his shirt hung in tatters. Paramedics carried a woman past him on a second stretcher. Thick honey blond hair blocked his view of her face. The color and texture of her hair jostled his memories.

Nee, he didn't have time to think of Katie now.

But then the woman on the second stretcher turned her head. He stared. That *Englisch* woman had his Katie's face. Older, *ja*, but he'd know those high cheekbones and that annoyingly adorable widow's peak anywhere. Without thinking, he stepped closer. "Katie? *Ist es du?*"

The bishop sucked in a surprised breath next to him.

Impossible, Abram told himself. He was being a fool. Then her eyes, those deep blue eyes, opened. They were vague and cloudy with pain before she looked straight at him.

"Abram," she murmured, her lids closing. "He looks just like Abram."

Abram couldn't believe she'd recognized him. The last time she'd seen him, he'd been a teenager, just past seventeen. That was over nine years ago. Almost ten. But maybe not so surprising. He'd recognized her almost the second he'd seen her.

"Excuse me." One of the paramedics edged in beside her stretcher. "On three." They lifted her into the ambulance. Abram watched, his mind dull with shock. The female paramedic climbed into the back with Katie while the man hopped into the cab behind the steering wheel. Abram backed out of the way to give them room to turn around. The ambulance drove past him, driving half on the lawn to pass the fire truck.

He'd known Katie had left. He didn't know she'd become *Englisch*. How did she know Beth?

The bishop had said that Beth wasn't really Amish. He gazed down the street, his mind grappling to comprehend that Katie was back, after all these years.

For her to show up here, now, was no coincidence. He was sure of it. What he didn't know was how her arrival and Beth's disappearance were connected.

TWO

"Abram."

The bishop. He'd forgotten that Bishop Hershberger was with him.

"Ja?"

"How do you know that woman?" He didn't hear disapproval, merely curiosity.

"Her name's Katie Bontrager. She used to be Amish." He faced the bishop, struggling to keep the myriad of emotions slamming around inside him off his face, although he couldn't control the flush warming his cheeks and ears. "We were friends when we were younger. After her parents were killed in an accident, she left the community. I never knew why."

The bishop's wise gaze speared him. It was difficult to stand still, but he managed. He braced himself for the bishop's questions. Abram wouldn't lie. If the bishop asked if he and Katie had been walking out together, he'd tell him yes, although they hadn't started officially courting. After all, she'd only been sixteen and hadn't joined in the singings yet. But they'd had a plan. As soon as she was seventeen and her *daed* said

she could attend the singings, he'd be there to drive
her home.

However, one day she was gone, no warning, no
explanations. Even her best friend, the bishop's wife,
Edith, had no clue where she'd gone. Or why. And his
dreams had died as his heart withered.

Had Edith told her husband about Katie? The man
gave no indication that he had ever heard of Katie Bontrager.

The bishop nodded and sighed. "Abram, I'm not
sure asking for your assistance with this matter was
a *gut* idea."

Abram startled. He stopped staring in the direction
the ambulances had gone and focused his attention
on the elder. "Bishop? You said that my experiences
would help."

"*Ja.* I did. Now that I know of your connection to
Kate, I am having second thoughts."

The bishop said her name as if he were acutely
aware of who Katie was. His stomach sank. Abram
glanced back over his shoulder again. The cloud of dust
caused by the speeding emergency vehicles had settled.

"Do you mean—"

"*Ja.* Kate Bontrager is one of the officers sent here
to investigate. I'm assuming the man with her was the
other officer we're expecting."

Abram opened his mouth to agree, to ask the bishop
to release him from his promise to assist. He paused.
This was his one chance to find out what had happened.
It wouldn't heal the breach between him and Katie.
Nothing could do that. The *maidel* he knew was gone
forever. However, maybe knowing the truth, confronting the issue and demanding answers, he could finally

be free of the bitterness that had curled up inside his heart since she'd left. If he could get past that, maybe he could let go of the past, once and for all.

Could he do it? Work with her, day by day? *Ja*. He could. The opportunity to know the truth outweighed any awkwardness that might ensue.

"*Nee*. I will help. The fact that I knew her once won't get in the way." He hoped. "Should we go to the hospital?"

Bishop Hershberger nodded. "*Ja*. I want to make sure they are well. And it would be *gut* to know if they learned anything new regarding Beth."

Abram grimaced. Did he want to go to the hospital? *Nee*, he did not. He wanted to go home to his quiet *haus*. His *mamm* was sure to have leftovers from dinner. He yearned to go home and eat some of his *mamm*'s *gut* cooking, read his Bible and go to bed. He didn't want to go to the hospital to see the woman who'd betrayed him and set off the series of events that had led to his bleak existence.

He'd already decided on his course, though. He needed to see it through.

He climbed back up in his buggy and waited for the bishop to join him. Once the other man was seated beside him, he grabbed the reins. Before he flicked them, he turned to look back at the *haus*. "What would cause damage like that?"

Bishop Hershberger shook his head. "*Ich weiß es nicht.*"

He didn't know, either. Nothing natural, he was fairly sure about that.

It didn't take them long to get to the hospital.

"We'll only stay a few minutes," the bishop said.

Twenty minutes later, the nurse said they could see Katie. The young man was still in surgery. The doctor wouldn't tell them any more than that since they weren't family. The bishop couldn't remember the other officer's name.

"I have it written down at home," he confided to Abram.

"Your friend Katie is awake," the doctor said. "She seems to be holding her own. We'll observe her overnight. If she has no other issues, she'll be released tomorrow morning."

The bishop thanked the doctor for his time. The doctor acknowledged them with a nod and departed.

"She's in room thirteen," the nurse said. "We're trying to find her family…"

"She has no family in the area," Abram blurted.

"None?"

He winced. Maybe she was married. "None that I know of," he amended his statement. "Her parents were both killed about nine and a half years ago. She has a couple of sisters, but I have no idea where. They both left the district after they married. I doubt she's been in contact with them in the past decade."

The nurse clucked her tongue. "That's a shame. She'll have to have someone to drive her home."

"*Ja*, we can take care of that," Bishop Hershberger replied. "She's coming to stay with us."

Abram blinked. The last he'd heard, Katie and the other officer were supposed to stay at the bed-and-breakfast. Apparently, the bishop had decided to change the arrangements.

Bishop Hershberger finished talking with the nurse

and walked toward Katie's room. Abram knew he was supposed to follow.

Slamming his fists into his pockets, Abram strode after the bishop. Entering Katie's room, he saw another patient sleeping in the first bed. He sidled past the elderly woman, taking care not to wake her. A curtain divided the two beds, blocking Abram's view of Katie. He stepped up to the edge of the curtain and halted, unwilling to go farther. His pulse hammered in his chest.

The bishop grabbed the chair next to the wall and dragged it to the end of the bed. He sat down as if this were nothing more than a normal visit to one of his congregation. "Katie Bontrager, ain't so?"

"Kate. I'm called Kate now."

He didn't know why that was painful for him to hear. She wasn't part of his world anymore. Many adults left their nicknames behind.

"Kate, then. We found you outside Beth Zook's *haus*." He lowered his voice. "You're one of the officers sent to find her, *ja*?"

A hurried rustling sound hit his ears. He heard her mutter frantically but didn't catch what she said. Without thinking, Abram stepped around the curtain. Katie, or Kate, was sitting up, tugging at the tape holding the IV in her arm. He hurried to her side and placed a hand on hers to stop her from removing the needle. The moment his hand touched her skin, she jerked away as if he'd burned her. Shocked, he stepped back. What had caused that reaction? It was almost like she were afraid of him.

Her gaze met his briefly before skittering away. His chest tightened at the angst he saw in her eyes. A tide of red spread up her neck and face. When she ducked her head, her long hair slipped forward and hid her features. He couldn't look away. He'd often wondered what it would look like down. The golden tresses fell to her shoulders. She'd had it cut since she left the community. It was still as lovely as he'd thought it would be.

Furious with himself, he wrenched his eyes away. *Nee*, this wasn't right. He should not be attracted to her. She was *Englisch* now. And she was here because someone was in danger.

"Katie…" His throat closed, blocking his words.

"What are you doing here?" The words were low, almost as if they'd been wrung from her.

"Ah," the bishop broke in. "Kate, young Abram is here on my request. I need his help and I have informed him of everything."

Abram cleared his throat. She was still fiddling with the IV.

"You almost died." His voice came out rough. "You need to leave the IV in."

She still wouldn't look at him. Instead, she turned her blue eyes to look at the bishop. "Where's Shane? Is he all right?"

"Your friend? He's still in surgery. I'm sure the doctor will tell you more later."

Her devastated expression tugged at his heart. Abram wanted to ask her about Shane. He knew the other man was probably her partner. Was he more than that? Perhaps a boyfriend? Her husband? He held the words in. He shouldn't care either way.

"He took the brunt of the blast." Her eyes were shiny. She blinked rapidly, glancing away. When she looked back, her control was in place again. She avoided his gaze and looked straight into the bishop's eyes. "You were correct. Shane and I are police officers from Wallmer Grove. He's my partner. We were sent here to go undercover and find Beth Zook."

Abram frowned. "You didn't look undercover. You were dressed *Englisch*."

Her mouth tightened. She jerked her head up to meet his gaze. "I have Amish clothes in the car we were driving. I planned on changing before I went to the bishop's house. Shane and I made a split-second decision to have a look around first." She shook her head, guilt painted on her expression. "No, that's not accurate. I asked Shane to stop. We wouldn't have been there if not for me."

"But someone else might have gone there."

Ack, it sounded like he was defending her. He definitely wasn't doing that.

She tilted her head, considering. "You're right, of course. I'd much rather risk my own life than that of someone else."

Bishop Hershberger leaned forward. "I'm sorry anyone was injured. Did you find anything at the Zook *haus*? Maybe something that could tell us where Beth is?"

Kate shook her head, her gaze sweeping between the men. The bleakness in her glance hit him like a clenched fist in the belly.

"Nothing. We didn't even get into the house. The porch exploded." She turned to the bishop. "Something like that is usually not an accident."

"You're right," a voice said behind him. Abram jumped. He'd been so focused on Katie, the man had snuck up on them. Turning his head, he watched a

Sutter Springs police officer step past the first bed
and head in their direction. "It wasn't an accident. It
was a bomb."

Of course, it was a bomb. She'd known that the second she heard the click that preceded the blast, which
had so nearly killed both Shane and her. Possibly a
pipe bomb. Something simple. It hadn't been strong
enough to be fatal, fortunately. She'd need to investigate the scene.

Kate fought the urge to chew on her lower lip. Never
show any sign of vulnerability. That was the rule she
lived her life by.

Except it was kind of hard not to look vulnerable
when lying in a hospital bed in a flimsy garment with
three men watching her. Her skin crawled as the new-
comer stepped closer into her space. *There is nothing wrong with the man*, she chided herself. He strode
nearer, confidence oozing from him, his expression
giving no hint of his thoughts. Law enforcement. She'd
have known even if he hadn't been in uniform. His rank
insignia said lieutenant.

"I'm Lieutenant Greer." He stared down at her. "I
just spoke to a doctor. Your friend is out of surgery.
It'll be tomorrow before he's coherent, but he should
live. He'll be here for a few days, maybe a week, to
recover. He has some serious burns."

Shane was going to be all right. She held on to that.
She'd also do her best to find the person responsible.
It had to be connected with Beth.

"Lieutenant," she greeted him. Something about
him rubbed her the wrong way, though she concealed
her instinct to inch away from him. "My name's Kate.

Kate Bontrager. Have you discovered who set the explosive?"

He narrowed his eyes, obviously not liking that she was asking questions.

"I haven't heard yet. What I would like to know is what you and your friend were doing there?"

She had to be careful. He might not know that she was a cop, or he might. Neither she nor Shane had carried their badges. Still, it would be easy enough for someone in law enforcement to get to the truth. Either way, she was sure that he wouldn't take kindly to cops from Wallmer Grove coming to Sutter Springs to investigate one of his townspeople who had gone missing. If he even knew. She doubted it. The Amish rarely asked *Englischers* for help. Especially *Englisch* law enforcement. She knew that personally. The only reason she'd been brought in was because Beth wasn't really Amish.

The chief said the US Marshals believed a crime ring was building up strength in the area. There were doubts as to how involved Beth might be, or if she was a victim. Kate needed to stay and complete her investigation.

Even if it meant breathing the same air as Abram.

She stiffened her shoulders. Her past with Abram wouldn't stop her. Never again would she allow a man to decide her fate. As long as she kept their relationship professional, all would be well.

"I'm visiting for a time." That was simple enough. Abram shifted. Unease skittered across his face, then disappeared. She might have missed it, if she hadn't once known him so well. He didn't give her away, so he probably understood that she was protecting her cover.

She hated undercover jobs. She had never been able to shake her mother's teachings about always being truthful. While she understood the reasons for the deception, it went against her character to lie.

A life is at stake.

The lieutenant scanned her face, her hair. His expression barely changed, but the unseen sneer emanated from him. What did he know?

"That's true." The bishop smiled vaguely.

"What's your purpose in visiting?" The lieutenant leaned closer.

Irritation bubbled up inside her. She was the victim here, not the perpetrator. Lieutenant Greer was treating her like a suspect.

"She used to live in the area," Abram broke in, startling her. "Her family's Amish."

She whipped her head around to stare at Abram.

Lieutenant Greer eyed her and Abram for a second.

"Sorry. With a name like Bontrager, that figures." He shrugged. "I didn't see your hair up, so I didn't connect that you were Amish. Guess I should have, with the bishop here visiting you."

She would have to wear her Amish disguise now. His manner eased as he continued with his questions. "How well did you know the woman who owned the house?"

She needed to tread lightly here. "Not very well. We'd met several years ago. I decided to visit her house as long as I was in the area."

That was true; Beth had still been Bailey when they'd met. She'd immediately felt a connection with the battered woman. They'd both survived horrific traumas.

"Did you see anyone hanging around or notice anything unusual?"

She shook her head. A few minutes later, he departed. As Abram shifted, her gaze had snagged on him. His jaw was smooth and clean-shaven. She'd been so focused on the explosion and Shane she hadn't realized the significance. He had never married. Amish men, once married, always wore a beard. Even a widower wouldn't shave his beard.

It wasn't any of her business. It was a shame, though. Abram was one of those men you knew would have been a great husband and father.

She was torn. Part of her was glad that he wasn't married. Which was ridiculous. She had never married, either. Although her reasons had to do with a terror-filled day that had nearly destroyed her.

A thought occurred to her. "Our car was parked at Beth's house. It might still be there with my clothes in it."

Bishop Hershberger smiled. "I'm sure we can get your belongings on our way here tomorrow."

She peered up at Abram. His face was blank. Did he resent helping her?

"Kate," Bishop Hershberger murmured.

She turned to the bishop. "Yes, sir?"

"I know we planned for you to stay at the Plain and Simple Bed and Breakfast. I would like to suggest a different plan. Tomorrow when you are released, I'd like you to come and stay with me and my *frau*."

Staying in the house of a bishop. Not if she could help it. It made her skin crawl to think of staying under the rule of an Amish house again. "I appreciate your invitation, but I'd like to still stay at the B&B. It would be a good place to start investigating, don't you think?"

"Bishop Hershberger, she may be right. That's where Beth worked, after all."

She glanced at Abram. "Did you know her?"

He shrugged. "Not well. But my family owns the B&B. I think they'd be able to answer some of your questions."

She nodded briefly at Abram to thank him. He wasn't looking at her. The bishop considered that. After a few moments, he agreed.

"*Ja*, that would be wise. I do expect you to *cumme* for supper. We have much to discuss. Beth's disappearance isn't the only troubling event lately." He leaned in and lowered his voice. "I went out to Beth's *haus* a few days ago. I knew she was gone. I prayed she would have returned, unharmed. I would have called her handler and told her that she had come back."

What was he telling her? Kate tensed in the hospital bed, clenching and releasing her fists. "Did you notice anything?"

He shook his head. "I didn't. I stood on her back porch, the same place you and your partner stood on today."

She caught her breath. "The bomb. It hadn't been placed yet."

Abram frowned. "So someone placed it, hoping to kill Beth?"

"Or whoever came looking for her," Kate muttered.

"*Ja*. That is what I thought, too," the bishop agreed.

"Katie, are you in danger?" Abram stared at her, his gaze so intense she had to avert her eyes.

It was a question worth considering. "If someone

has figured out who Beth really is, maybe the bomb wasn't directly targeting me."

Other than being a cop, what reason would anyone have to target her? Unease danced down her spine. She suppressed a shudder. The sooner this case was over, the sooner she could leave.

Impatient, she waved her hand, dismissing the subject. Worrying never solved anything. "I'll be fine. I doubt that bomb had anything to do with me."

"Then we'll leave you to get some rest," Bishop Hershberger declared, pushing himself to his feet. He nodded to her and excused himself.

Frustrated, she watched him. She still had questions. Obviously, she wouldn't get answers today. Her gaze shot to Abram. He shrugged and strode after the bishop, leaving her alone with her thoughts.

She huffed. Really, they were leaving after giving her a morsel like that to chew on? Who was the target? She had no idea what other stuff they were referring to. It might be the issues the captain had mentioned. Or it could be entirely new information.

Either way, she hated the idea of stewing over what the bishop could have meant until the next day. The patient in the other bed was moved out soon after the bishop and Abram departed, leaving Kate in the room by herself. Her glance flicked to the window. The sunlight filtered through the blinds.

Despite her claims to being fine and in no danger, being alone in a hospital room in Sutter Springs gave her an itchy feeling all over.

The medication the nurse had given her was starting to make her feel sleepy. She fought it for a few minutes. Falling into a medicine-induced sleep made her vulnerable.

She couldn't take it anymore. Throwing her legs over the side of the bed, she steadied herself and yanked the IV out of her arm. She was fine. Her clothes, battered and singed, were folded on a tray next to her. They were better than wearing a thin hospital robe. Quickly, she dressed, frowning at the sorry state of her favorite jeans. Her jacket was too torn to wear. She wrinkled her nose at the blood on its sleeve. Nope. She tossed it into the trash can, wishing she had brought a warmer shirt.

Shrugging it off as unimportant, she stood and headed to the door.

She made it three steps when the door was thrust open. A large man entered the room, sliding a knife out from inside his leather jacket. She halted and backed up.

All questions about whether she was a target or not had been answered.

THREE

Kate continued to shift backward as the enormous stranger advanced into the room. She had no weapon. Her service revolver had been in her hand when she'd approached Beth's house. She had no idea where it was now.

"What were you doing, sniffing around her house?"

Her house? Did he mean Beth or Bailey? How much did this man know? Certainly, given the question, he'd seen Kate at the house.

"Who are you?" she countered his question with one of her own.

His expression darkened and he moved closer. She could smell his breath now and forced down the urge to gag. Not because of the smell. No, it was a visceral reaction to his closeness.

"Where is Beth?"

His question reassured her that he didn't know Beth Zook was really Bailey St. Andrews.

Think, Kate. Think.

There was nowhere to hide in this room. She briefly considered the alarm button attached to the control on the bed. She looked at the length of his legs and immediately discarded the idea. She'd have to turn her back on him, but he'd outrun her. She'd never make it to the alarm in time.

She sucked in a deep breath, preparing to yell for help.

"You make a sound, and whoever comes in dies."

She choked back the scream. The look in his eyes told her he meant what he said. She would not put a civilian life at risk. She had to find out what he wanted. Why had he come after her?

"We're going to go for a walk," he grated out. "No funny business. No calling for help, or trying to call attention to yourself. I have no problem killing anyone who gets in my way."

She believed him. It was a good thing she'd decided to get dressed. She'd run if she got the opportunity once they were away from others who could get hurt in her escape attempt.

A meaty hand reached out and grabbed her left elbow. He tugged her forward and forced her to walk in front of him through the door.

It took all her will not to resist him. Only the knowledge that lives were at stake if she breathed wrong kept her moving calmly along the hallway beside him. They passed a patient walking through the hall with an IV pole and a nurses' aide pushing a cart of used dinner trays. He took her in the opposite direction of the nurses' station. When they arrived at the elevator, her stomach flipped inside her.

She was going to be in that little box with only him. Sweat broke out on her forehead. She could feel her heart banging inside her chest. The elevator doors whooshed open. He pulled her inside.

"Hold that door!"

A hand flashed out and caught the door before it closed. The intern it belonged to smiled at them and stepped inside, followed by a young female aide. They stood in front of Kate and the male intern gabbed away about his fantasy football stats for the week. As glad as she was to not be alone with her captor, Kate was terrified for the unsuspecting pair. Tension vibrated from the man beside her. She held her breath, waiting for him to leap into action and take down the unsuspecting couple. He could do it. Of that she had no doubt. He was big and buff and an air of menace hovered around him like a thick cloud.

The elevator stopped with a jarring short jolt. She swayed with the movement. Chills broke out along her spine when her captor grasped her arm above the elbow and gave her a slight push. He didn't say a word. He didn't need to. She understood. Kate swallowed and followed the unsuspecting intern and aide out of the elevator. They turned down a hallway leading to the labs.

Kate obeyed the pressure on her arm and marched past the registration desk and through the sliding glass doors to the parking lot. Without moving her head, she shifted her eyes from side to side, scanning the area for a way to make her escape. An elderly man was close by, assisting his wife to their vehicle. A couple of teenagers were hanging out near an old pickup truck. A country song blared through the open window.

There were too many innocents about. She'd need to make sure that they didn't get harmed in any bid for freedom she made.

And she would make one. There was no way she was

going to get into a vehicle with this man. She'd never make it out alive. Was he the one after her?

She dismissed that thought. He might have set the bomb. He might have even done something to Bailey/Beth. But her gut said this was not the person behind it all. A quick glance up at his smooth expression confirmed her thoughts. No, more likely he was a hired gun, someone paid to get rid of any risks.

To whom had Beth posed a risk?

And why was she, Kate, considered a risk?

The old man and his wife exited the lot in a sleek four-door sedan. The teens were still there.

A few seconds later, one of them called out, "Dude, you've been in there forever!"

A lone kid strolled over, his left arm in a sling.

"I had to wait my turn. Good news is, the arm's not broken. Ready to roll?"

He joined his buddies amid laughs and jeers, and the group split up into two vehicles, the truck and a small sedan with mud splattered all over the side doors. Within seconds, the car pealed out of the lot. The truck, its engine roaring, followed after them.

No one was around.

Now was her chance, possibly her only opportunity to escape.

Mr. Menace stopped beside a dark blue Jeep Cherokee and threw open the back door and shoved her forward. Uh-uh. She dug in her heels and struggled to pull free from his grasp.

One large hand grabbed her arm and squeezed while his other muscled forearm shot to hold her around the neck and practically lifted her off her feet as he dragged her to the open door of the car. His grip was tight, but she was still able to breathe.

Swinging her feet wildly, Kate kicked back, hoping to hit his shins. Her boots had solid heels on them. If she could gouge him, it would hurt, maybe enough that he would drop her or loosen his grip. His arm tightened around her neck, cutting off her ability to scream.

Spots began to dance in front of her eyes. She was quickly losing the battle to break free. If he managed to get her into the Jeep, she'd be out of choices.

She was too young to die.

Abram walked down the hallway and paused before Katie's room. Now that he was here, he felt like a fool. He'd dropped the bishop off, then had come straight back, planning to talk with Katie privately without the bishop around. He'd been determined to ask her why she'd left. Taking in a deep breath, he stepped into Katie's room and came to a dead stop.

She was gone. He frowned. She had no clothes other than the tattered rags she'd been wearing when she was brought in. Surely, she wouldn't leave in those. They weren't decent, not with the holes and bloodstains on them.

Maybe she was in the restroom. He marched over to the door and knocked softly.

The door wasn't closed all the way.

It was dark inside the little room. He flipped on the light to make sure she wasn't passed out on the floor.

It was empty.

Spinning in a slow circle, a chilling thought entered his mind. Maybe she was a bit muzzy-headed from the medication or her wounds. She could be wandering about. He recalled one of the men from his family's painting business had fallen from a ladder and hit his head. No one had realized how hurt he really was until he'd walked in front of an oncoming car, completely unaware of the danger.

The man was fine now, but he could have been seriously injured or killed had he been alone.

Alone like Katie was.

Rushing from the room, Abram stood in the hall and swung his head to the left and right, searching for anyone who might be able to help him. A nurse was leaving a room farther down the hall.

Abram strode toward her, intent on discovering where Katie had disappeared to. The nurse saw him marching up to her and backed up, eyes wide. He forced his face to rearrange itself into a smile.

"Excuse me. I'm searching for my friend. Katie, um…Kate Bontrager? She was in room thirteen?"

Her expression cleared. "Oh, yes! The doctor must have discharged her. She left not more than five minutes ago."

"Left?" He felt a frown settling on his face again. "By herself? Did she say anything?"

She was already shaking her head. "Oh, she wasn't by herself. There was a man with her. I think they must have been arguing, because she was looking angry." A sudden blush swarmed up her cheeks. "I shouldn't be gossiping like this. Please excuse me."

Abram barely heard her. He knew Katie wouldn't have left with anyone. Her partner was here, and she didn't know anyone else to contact other than himself and the bishop.

She was in trouble.

Whirling around, he took off at a run toward the elevator, ignoring the nurse's startled yell behind him. Arriving at the elevator, he punched the button twice. Nothing. It was on the ground floor. Tapping his foot against the floor, he waited. When the door finally opened, it was full. A patient on a wheeled bed and a full slate of medical personnel stared out at him.

"Sorry, buddy. You'll have to catch it on the way down," one of them told him as the doors began to close.

Kate might not have time for him to wait for all of them to exit on the third floor and send the elevator back.

He spun and ran to the door leading to the stairs. Swinging it open, he charged down the steps, making no attempt to mask his presence. The air rang with the sound of his boots hitting the metal steps. If Katie was on the steps, she and whoever had her would hear him coming. He didn't pause, his entire being focused on finding Katie and making sure she was safe.

He burst from the stairwell and found himself near the hospital's main lobby. A young man in a white coat jumped back, exclaiming as he spilled hot coffee down the front of his coat. Idly, Abram wondered if he was old enough to be a doctor.

"Hey! Watch where you're going, man. This is a hospital."

"*Ja!* My friend was here, but she just left with someone. Blond hair, blue eyes, ragged clothes." He recalled her face. "A large bruise on her cheek and a cut on her forehead."

"Oh, yeah. I rode the elevator down with her a few minutes ago. She was heading out, I'm sure."

"I think she was kidnapped!" Abram exclaimed and then he was off again.

He exited the building at a run, aware of a commotion in his wake. He ignored it. Outside, he slowed to look around. *Please, Gott, let her still be here.*

A scream rent the air. *Katie!* Relief and alarm spurted through his veins, drumming in his ears.

He sprinted through the parking lot. When he saw her struggling in the arms of a man intent on forcing her in a Jeep, Abram pumped his arms for a final burst of speed. The man had her lifted partially off the ground and was trying to shove her into the vehicle feetfirst.

"Hey!" Abram bellowed.

Surprised, Katie's captor jerked around, dragging her kicking feet back out of the car.

Abram was almost there.

A commotion at the hospital door caught his attention. Security officers were running their way. With a growl, the stranger tossed Katie at him and jumped into the front seat, not even bothering to shut the back door. Abram's arms closed about Katie as they stumbled back, falling into a pile on the blacktop. The Jeep squealed away. Abram pulled Katie closer to the ground to avoid getting clipped by the swinging door. It slammed shut as the Jeep careened onto the road, nearly barreling into a minivan coming from the opposite direction.

Horns blared as the Jeep sped off.

Hands reached down and pulled them to their feet.

A few steps away, a security officer was calling in the incident, his voice hard and sharp.

A red-faced officer was standing next to Abram. It was the guard who'd been sitting behind the registration desk as Abram had dashed past. Perhaps he felt guilty for not knowing the woman was being abducted. He'd be in trouble, no doubt. Abram was too busy checking Katie for further injuries to waste time feeling sorry for the *Englischer*. She was shaking, but her eyes were clear.

"Katie? Are you well? Did he hurt you?" She was so pale he was half-afraid she'd go into shock.

Abram searched for additional injuries. Her neck was red and there was a bruise forming on her left arm near her elbow. Other than that, she appeared fine. Her eyes and lips were tight, but the gaze she sent his way was clear and didn't waver. Suddenly, her head snapped around toward the hospital. Tension radiated down the length of her.

"I'm fine. But did anyone check on Shane? That guy definitely came after me because I was at Beth's earlier today."

Within three seconds, they were surrounded by more security officers. One of them phoned into the hospital to have Shane checked out. Within a minute, they received word that he was fine and was still unconscious from the anesthesia.

"Can you describe your kidnapper, miss?" The man who'd called in the situation was off the phone and at her side.

"Yeah. About six foot four or five, probably around 240 pounds. He had short straight black hair, a beard, no visible scars or tats, and was wearing steel-toe boots, blue jeans and a black T-shirt with no logos or images on it. He drove a Jeep Cherokee, dark blue. I didn't get the license plate number."

They all turned and stared at her. It struck Abram that her monotone recitation of details probably sounded like a cop.

"*Ack*, you always did have a great eye for small details," he said.

She startled, as if only remembering her cover story. He took the grimace she tossed his way as a silent thanks.

"True."

He read the relief in her eyes. "Katie, I don't know what your plan is, but I'm wondering if we could go and visit the bishop?"

She was silent for a moment before nodding slowly. "That might be a good idea. But first, I want to see my friend, Abram."

He nodded. If Shane had been his friend, he'd want to see for himself that he was unharmed.

"*Ja*, we'll make sure he's okay before going to see the bishop." He searched her face, amazed she could be so calm after such a close call.

Katie looked so young in her jeans and T-shirt they might have concluded she was a young Amish girl going through her *Rumspringa*, or the time of running around. It is a time when some of the strictures are eased and young people are allowed more freedom so they may decide to join the Amish church or leave and enter the *Englisch* world.

He never bothered to take advantage of that time. Mostly because of the woman in front of him.

She was in danger. He couldn't abandon her, even

if the bishop hadn't charged him with her care. Some-one had already tried to get to her.

He'd help her. Then he'd let her go again.

For now, he had to guard his heart. He wasn't sure he would survive if she broke it again.

FOUR

The hospital staff and paramedics hovered around them like a swarm of bees around a hive. Kate edged closer to Abram and away from the strangers clustered around her. The noise was overwhelming. So many questions and voices talking at the same time. It was absurd to feel claustrophobic. She was a cop. She'd been in tight situations before.

But not like this. Overwhelmed by her memories of the past, having been nearly killed and then kidnapped at knifepoint in such a brief amount of time, she needed space to process it all so she could focus.

Space she wasn't likely to get. Abram was her only source of calm in this chaos. Leaning on him was not a good option. She was a bit fragile at the moment and she needed to be strong.

Forcing herself to move away from Abram, she moved closer to the paramedics, balking when a new one joined them with a wheelchair.

"I'm perfectly able to walk on my own." She felt a flush stain her cheeks. When they wouldn't budge, she lowered herself into the wheelchair with a disgusted sigh. Feeling vulnerable, she allowed herself to be led back into the hospital. Abram apparently wasn't willing to be left behind. He jogged back up to stand beside her.

"Did he demand you get dressed?" he whispered out of the side of his mouth. She'd forgotten that trick. His lips barely moved. Casting her gaze up, his eyes met hers, a glimmer of a question in them.

She'd have to come clean.

"I was just getting ready to walk out," she whispered back. "Being stuck in the hospital to wait when I was fine was a waste of time."

A soft sound, almost a snort left him. "Fine? You barely survived being blown up."

"Jetzt nicht," she whispered, telling him now was not the time for this particular conversation. There were too many people around. She was sort of surprised that she'd recalled the words; she hadn't spoken Pennsylvania Dutch, the German-based dialect her family and the other Amish used, in nine years. The words, however, had felt natural on her tongue.

He narrowed his eyes, but nodded. *"Ja."*

It was a promise. He would back down, but only for the moment. Later, he would demand to know everything. Her eyes flashed away from his, her heart pounding. Being nearly kidnapped had been terrifying. The idea of explaining herself to Abram Burkholder after all these years was less scary, but still daunting.

For the second time in less than twenty-four hours, Kate endured doctors prodding and poking at her while Lieutenant Greer showed up. He waited until the doctor declared she had suffered no further injuries and left to write her release papers before stepping closer to interrogate her.

"What did he want with you?" he barked at her,

scowling at her as if being taken against her will was all her idea.

Kate was all for being thorough, and she even understood being tough on a witness or a suspect. However, she had been nearly kidnapped from her hospital room. She was done being nice.

"I've already told you I don't know." She crossed her arms across her chest and frowned back at him. Abram stepped up next to her shoulder in a show of support. Surprised, she switched her gaze to him. Her former friend was almost glaring at the lieutenant, his eyes fierce and angry.

"Katie is the victim here, Lieutenant."

Wow. In all the years they'd grown up together, she had never heard him snap like that. Abram was always calm and deliberate. Always thoughtful. Almost remote. Who would have guessed that he would have the ability to speak to an authority figure like that?

She didn't know who he was anymore. It saddened her to realize that she didn't know what experiences had shaped him into the man he was now.

Belatedly, she realized he'd called her Katie. It wasn't the time to correct him. A small part of her liked the sound of her former nickname falling from his lips. In the chaos surrounding them, it was something familiar to ground her. Surely, it couldn't hurt to allow him this one small thing. Besides, Katie was a very common appellation among the Amish. Anyone she encountered who knew her from before was certain to call her that. If she corrected them all, it would raise more questions than it was worth. She'd let the matter lie.

The lieutenant held up his hands. "That may be so.

But the paramedics on the scene of the explosion found these." He pulled out a clear plastic bag. Inside them were two service weapons. She and Shane had dropped their guns when the house exploded. "These are police-issued weapons. You want to tell me the truth?"

All he'd have to do was look up the numbers on the guns. Had he already done that? She couldn't lie, but maybe she didn't have to tell him the entire truth.

"I'm a police officer from Wallmer Grove. So is my partner, Shane Pearson."

His eyes narrowed and he opened his mouth. She rushed on before he could ask any more questions. "I did grow up in this area. Shane and I were on our way to visit the bishop and I asked if we could stop by Beth's house first."

All true. Sort of.

"Let's say I believe you. But this whole situation is wrong. You show up at a house and nearly get yourself blown up. Then I hear from one of the guys at the office that the girl you were visiting hasn't shown up for work and is missing."

She exchanged glances with Abram. They kept quiet and listened to the lieutenant rant.

"Now I'm called back the same day to find you've been nearly abducted and held at knifepoint. Would someone like to tell me the truth? How do you know the missing woman?"

Balling her hands into fists to keep them steady, she pressed them against her sides. "I met Beth several years ago. When I decided to come home, I stopped by her house. It didn't look like she was home, so we decided to knock on the door. You know what happened next."

"Yes." The word was drawn out. She didn't like the sound of it. "You said it didn't look like anyone was home, right? Why would you assume there was trouble? I'm guessing you had your weapons out, since they weren't found in the car or on your person."

Wincing, Kate thought fast. How could she explain? The only option she could see would be to talk with Lieutenant Greer alone and answer his questions. Except Beth was a federal witness. Giving details about her might get Kate into a heap of trouble. Lieutenant Greer probably wouldn't like it if she asked him to let her call her captain first before she answered any more questions.

"I'm afraid your questions cannot be answered at this time," a deep male voice said.

Kate, Abram and the police lieutenant all turned at this new voice. Two strangers entered the room and closed the door. The man was in his early forties with red hair and serious brown eyes gleaming behind wire-framed glasses. The woman looked to be in her mid- to late-thirties. She wore light makeup, and her hair was pinned up in some sort of fancy twist. Except for her clothes, she seemed very feminine in a modern way. Both wore dark trousers and jackets. At the same time, they reached inside their jackets and whipped out badges. Federal badges. The man spoke.

"I'm Marshal Tim Hendrix, and this is Marshal Amy Delacure. I'm sorry, Lieutenant. This case is the jurisdiction of the US Marshals."

Speculation grew on Lieutenant Greer's face. Kate glanced at Abram and rolled her eyes. He gave her a crooked half smile back. Not flirtatiously. He was telling her he agreed with her assessment of the situation.

By announcing that the case belonged to the Marshals, the newcomers had all but shouted that there was much more going on than Kate was telling.

However, that also removed the lieutenant's need to question her and Shane. Which could be a good thing. Either way, what was done was done.

"You know, that just makes me all the more curious," he retorted.

Marshal Delacure shrugged, a sympathetic smile on her face. "Yes, we know. Can't be helped, though. I'm sure you understand."

A muffled chuckle came from Abram. When she looked at him, though, his face was devoid of all emotion. He gave her a sidewise glance and a wink. She remembered that look. Abram was amused. Probably, like her, he knew a facetious remark when he heard it, even if it was sugarcoated and said with a sweet smile and southern drawl.

Greer jammed his hat back on his head and made to leave.

"Before you go," Marshal Hendrix said, a pleasant smile on his face that didn't reach his eyes. "I think it would be a good idea to let Officer Bontrager have her property back. And release her car, while you're at it."

Greer fumed and handed the bag over before he left. He did not look happy. Kate didn't blame him. He had every right to suspect her. She was glad to have her gun returned to her, though.

Delacure turned her eyes to Abram. Before she could tell him to leave, Kate blurted, "He's part of this. The bishop has made him my liaison, so to speak."

Why had she done that? If she'd kept quiet, the marshals would have demanded he leave. But what would have been the point? He already knew everything.

And she wanted him to stay.

She flinched away from that thought. Her life had gotten way too complicated recently. If she grew close to him once more, she would be putting her heart at risk again.

Kate rubbed her throat where her captor's arm had strangled her.

If she weren't careful, she'd also be putting his life, and those around him, in jeopardy, too.

She'd walk away again before that happened.

If she could.

Abram didn't like the way she kept rubbing her throat. Seeing that man attempting to force her into his vehicle brought one thing home to Abram. Even after nearly ten years, part of his heart, at the very least, still belonged to Katie. Who knew how she felt?

He had to get past that. He was Amish, and she wasn't. His commitment was to *Gott*, not to her. If he wanted to ever be able to marry and have *kinder* of his own, he needed to move on.

But first, he needed to know that she was safe.

The marshals didn't appear pleased that she insisted he remain. Surprisingly, they didn't resist, other than to aim a dark look or two at him.

Marshal Hendrix scowled. "I don't like it. But if he's already in the know, I guess it would be a good idea to keep him close."

Abram almost rolled his eyes. Like he'd spill their secrets to anyone.

"We need to take this conversation to a more secure location," Marshal Delacure interrupted him.

Without a word, Marshal Hendrix exited the examination room. Katie bit her lip, but refrained from saying anything. Abram was content to watch this new development play out. He'd learned long ago that observation could often tell you more than talking. A few awkward minutes later, Marshal Hendrix returned with a doctor, a distinguished looking fellow in his midfifties or so.

"I have a conference room you can use."

Katie was off the examination table before he'd finished speaking, relief on her face.

The doctor led them down the hall. Abram and Katie picked up the rear, walking behind the marshals. Neither of them said a word. He suspected she was occupied with trying to hear what the marshals were saying, like he was. Abram didn't like being kept in the dark on something this important. When Marshal Hendrix kept up a litany of whispered complaints to his partner, Abram glanced down at Katie. Raising an eyebrow, he pointed at the lawman. She shrugged and shook her head in response to his silent, *What's up with him?* question.

When they arrived at their destination, the doctor moved aside and gestured for them to enter. Abram stepped in behind Katie. A blast of cold air hit his face.

"Wow, it's like winter in here." Katie shivered.

He frowned, wishing he had a jacket to offer her. All she had was her T-shirt. He could see the raised bumps on her arms.

The inquisition started again.

"I don't like—" Marshal Hendrix began.

"It's done." Marshal Delacure shrugged again. "What I want to know is how they broke your cover so fast?"

"I'm not sure that they did," Katie said slowly. She shook her head and frowned. "I don't think the explosion was meant for us. I don't know whom it was meant for, or who set it. But I plan to find out."

"What makes you so sure?"

"Just a feeling."

"And the guy who almost nabbed you?" Marshal Delacure took a seat at the large rectangular table. They all followed suit.

Katie bit her lip and squinted her eyes in thought. "When he came in, he asked me how I knew Beth. I don't think he knew I was a cop. More likely, someone is searching for Beth and was watching the house."

Marshal Hendrix leaned in. "Did he make any mention of your police work?"

"No. His whole focus was on Beth. So obviously he wasn't involved in her disappearance."

"Maybe not her disappearance, but I'm curious to know why he was watching for her." Marshal Hendrix sat back, drumming his fingers on the table.

"What was she doing?" Katie burst out. "Was she involved in something she shouldn't have been?"

As far as he could tell, these were rhetorical questions.

Except Marshal Delacure looked uneasy. "I don't know if it means anything, but she seemed very distracted the last time we met. We were in Berlin at a coffee shop. Just having a casual lunch. She mentioned a young boy that had recently overdosed, but then the waitress brought our food. When she left, Beth changed the subject."

Abram pushed his chair back and stood so he could pace. The others stared at him, but he ignored them. He needed to think. "I think I know who she was talking about. There was a boy who died recently. He was in another district, so I'm not sure of his name. It was real suspicious, though. Everyone who knew him declared he'd never been involved with anything like drugs before."

"I'm not sure what you mean by he isn't from your district. I don't know why everyone was shocked. Isn't that a normal thing, with your running around time, whatever it's called? I think you'd expect something like this if you let your kids ignore the rules."

Abram scowled. Who was this man to judge their customs?

"It's called *Rumspringa*, and you have no clue what you're talking about." Katie bit out each word. "How did you become Beth's handler if you aren't familiar with Amish culture?"

"He's not. I am." Marshal Delacure glared at her partner. "We are together because there's safety in numbers."

"To answer your question," Abram said, mostly to diffuse the thick tension vibrating in the room, "the Amish community is divided into districts. There are around nineteen families in each. That makes it easier to gather. Most of the districts have their own bishop, preachers and deacons. Although there are a couple of districts that share a bishop."

"And *Rumspringa* doesn't mean all the rules disappear," Katie added. "Sure, some of the rules are more relaxed, but most kids don't do much. So, no. Having a kid suddenly do a one-eighty and start taking drugs is not normal."

Marshal Hendrix sighed. "I apologize. I think we need to assume that this case might be connected to her disappearance."

"How do you mean?" Katie asked in a soft voice.

"I mean, maybe Beth was somehow involved in what happened."

Marshal Delacure's mouth tightened. "I don't believe it, Tim. You didn't know her like I did."

He looked at her, his eyes softening. "I'm sorry, Amy. But is it possible you didn't know her the way you thought you did? If you had, why didn't she complete the story? I would have thought she'd have confided in you."

The woman was tormenting herself. Blaming herself. Abram sat again. "I don't mean to interrupt, but I don't think you should blame yourself. You aren't responsible for another person's actions. None of us is. Even with parents and children. You can try to teach them the right way, but at some point, they have to be allowed to make their own choices and deal with the consequences. That's all part of the free will *Gott* gave us."

Katie jolted upright, like he'd hit her with a cattle prod. Her face was pale.

Something had really upset her.

"You all right?" For just a second, he ignored the others in the room, all his attention zeroed in on her.

She nodded. She wasn't, but he understood. She wouldn't say whatever she thought here, in front of these two marshals. He had to respect that.

The marshals were both watching.

Katie's face went blank. "So, we know she disappeared, although we don't know how or why. Or if she left on her own or had help. We also know we're not the only ones looking for her."

Amy Delacure nodded. "As much as I hate to admit it, we also have to consider that she might have gotten herself into trouble that has nothing to do with her being a witness."

"You thought she'd been found by whomever she was running from." Abram rubbed his chin. "That could have put my family and friends in danger."

His voice was mild, but his mood was not. How dare these *Englischers* endanger his community this way? He wasn't sure how he felt about Katie's involvement in this. It was almost another betrayal.

"If a witness follows instructions, the danger is minimal."

He curled his lip at Marshal Hendrix. Easy for him to say.

"Abram," Katie said. She attempted to smile. Her lips trembled slightly. "I get why you're mad. I do. But right now, we have to find Beth. I agree that she isn't in danger from the people from her past. As far as I know, they're all still in jail. But a woman is still missing and might be in serious danger. I hope she's still alive, although there's a chance we're already too late to save her. We have to work together to find her."

His glare encompassed them all. "I will continue to help because my bishop has asked me to. But know this—" his gaze landed on Katie and stayed "—I will not stand by and let any harm come to my family or my neighbors. No matter what orders I have been given."

FIVE

Silence descended on the room. He tightened his jaw, daring them to argue.

They didn't. A knock on the door broke through the heavy silence.

The door opened and the doctor who had shown them to the conference room entered. His gaze zeroed in on Katie. "I thought you should be aware that your friend is awake."

Katie shot out of her chair. "Shane's awake? Is he okay?"

"He will be. He's in a lot of pain right now, and his meds will keep him groggy for a bit. I need to know who to contact." His gaze slid over to Marshal Hendrix.

Marshal Hendrix stood and ushered the doctor out of the room.

"They'll tell his wife, won't they?" Katie demanded, whirling to face Marshal Delacure.

Abram blinked. Shane was married. He wasn't happy with how relieved that thought made him. He had no right feeling happy knowing she and the young officer she'd come to Sutter Springs with weren't a couple. No right at all.

"They'll notify her, but they won't be able to tell her what he was doing or anything about the case he was working on."

Katie seemed to accept that. When she was allowed to finally see her partner later that afternoon, Abram waited for her with Marshal Hendrix. If he'd had his druthers, he'd have gone with them, not liking letting her out of his sight. He didn't put up a fuss, though. There was no point.

One good thing about Marshal Hendrix. The man wasn't chatty. He set up a small laptop on the table and sat next to Abram in the conference room working. When the women reentered the room, he greeted them with a grunt and continued tapping away at the keys.

"Everything *gut*?" Abram asked.

"Fine." Katie smiled. She looked exhausted. The skin under her eyes was blue with fatigue. "They said he'll be able to continue working in a couple of days."

"Maybe we should send you two home and bring another pair of officers in." Finally, Marshal Hendrix spoke.

"Not necessary," Marshal Delacure said, pouring herself a glass of water. When she lifted the pitcher in question, both Abram and Katie declined. "It doesn't seem either attacks were aimed at Kate because of her cover. For the time being, I think the benefits of her familiarity with the people and the area outweigh the cons."

"Fine." Marshal Hendrix snapped his laptop closed and stood. Abram was shocked that he let the matter go without argument. Apparently, he trusted Marshal Delacure's judgment. "You'll keep us informed if you need anything or if there are any issues."

It wasn't a question.

Katie nodded. "I will. I have the cell phone that my captain gave me still. I'll use it if I need to."

"How will you recharge it?" Marshal Hendrix asked.

Abram responded. "She'll be staying at the bed-and-breakfast. Since they cater to *Englischers* wanting to see Amish life, there will be electricity in her room."

As they walked out, Abram noticed a bag with Kate's name on it sitting at the nurses' station. "I nearly forgot. Lieutenant Greer said you could have your belongings back. He must have sent your clothes and such."

No one paid him any attention as he grabbed the bag and handed it to Katie.

She took it, jerking it out of his hands when his fingers brushed hers. He reeled back a step, stunned by the electricity that had jolted him when their skin touched.

This was wrong on so many levels.

She ducked into a restroom to change. Restless, he watched the marshals depart. When did his life get this complicated? *Mamm* and *Daed* might not appreciate his getting involved with the *Englisch* law. Although, what could they say since it was Bishop Hershberger's decision?

He heard the sound of boots on the floor behind him, a soft quick step. Turning, he blinked, stunned. His mouth dried up. The *Englisch* Katie he'd seen a few minutes before was gone. She now looked exactly how he'd imagined Amish Katie would look all grown up.

She had always loved pink. The deep rose-colored dress suited her. Katie had tucked her lovely honey blond hair under a white prayer *kapp*, leaving only the front two inches visible. Proper Amish women kept their hair covered, only letting their husbands and family see it down. It felt strange that he'd seen it. He remembered what that hair looked like around her shoulders. He brought himself sharply back to the present. She was not really Amish. She was a woman who had chosen to leave the Amish world without a word to anyone. Not even to him, the man who'd planned on marrying her.

He couldn't forget that. Not ever.

"Ready to go?" He hadn't meant for his voice to be so abrupt.

"Sure am." She stood and walked to him, her face closed. Even though she was dressed Amish, she was still every inch an *Englisch* officer. Turning from her, he led the way out to where his buggy was still parked. It was a typical buggy with two seats inside. One in back and the other in front with a window for the driver to hold the reins and control the horses. She scrambled up into buggy before he could offer to help her and moved into the back seat. For a second, he stared, startled.

He had assumed they'd ride side by side. She'd taken that decision right out of his hands, making it clear that even though they were working together, that was all this was. A temporary partnership.

Still. It felt odd having her in the back while he drove.

"I don't want anyone to see me." Her voice floated out to him. "Not yet."

Right. If he was seen driving her to the bishop's *haus*, it might cause rumors and speculation that would be best avoided.

So maybe she wasn't avoiding him.

He hopped up onto the bench in front and took the

reins into his hands, clicking his tongue against the roof of his mouth and flicking his wrists. He swayed when the horse began to move, planting his boots firmly on the floor to keep his balance.

It wasn't that far from the hospital to the bishop's *haus*. When he arrived, he pulled around back.

"We're at the bishop's *haus*," he called softly.

She popped out of the buggy. "Why are we here, anyway? I know we talked about it at the hospital, but I wasn't sure why you wanted to stop here when I'm supposed to stay at the bed-and-breakfast."

"Ja." He started walking toward the steps. She fell in beside him. Casting a glance to the woman at his side, he smiled at her. She was tugging on the ends of her *kapp* straps, the way she always did when she was impatient. She was adorable. At least she wasn't chewing on them, the way his young cousin did.

She huffed. "Well?"

He chuckled. He'd never answered her question. "The bishop wanted a word with you before you went there, and I said I'd bring you by."

She nodded. "In that case—"

Her words died away as the door opened with a crash. Edith, the bishop's *frau*, stood there staring at Katie, gasping. "Katie, *bist du das*?"

Katie blanched. Her lips trembled as she moved closer to the woman. He'd forgotten to warn her that Edith had married Bishop Hershberger. He'd known that Edith and Katie had once been friends.

"Yes, it's me." Her body was stiff when she halted in front of Edith.

The wooden expression on her face bothered him. Clearly, she expected to be rebuffed. Instead, Edith cried out and swallowed her in a tight embrace, swaying from side to side.

"I can't believe it! You left us, no word! Was it because of—"

Katie's hand shot up and covered the woman's mouth. Edith's eyes widened. Both women glanced at him, then back at each other.

Abram narrowed his eyes and bounced them back and forth between the two women. Edith knew something. Something that had ended in Katie leaving her Amish life, and him, behind.

What was it? And why hadn't she felt she could trust him enough to tell him? And why hadn't he noticed something was going on that was bad enough for her to abandon her entire life?

Had she failed him, or had he failed her?

"Cumme." Edith backed away from her old friend and motioned for them both to enter the *haus*. "There is much to discuss. Are you hungry? I know it's getting late, but I would be happy to make you something to eat before you go to the Plain and Simple Bed and Breakfast."

Abram removed his hat and placed it on a hook inside the door. He didn't want to stay. Being so close to Katie was hard enough. The events of the day, though, were starting to take their toll on his mental state. He needed to be doing something physical to help him deal with the unease crawling under his skin.

Katie had almost died. Possibly twice.

How could she be so calm? It was the nature of her job; he understood that. But the violence she must see on a regular basis—what did that do to your soul?

As soon as this case was done, she'd be going back

to that life. Did anyone really have her back there? He scanned her face as she laughed with Edith. Did Edith see the deep sadness in her gaze, the way she was holding herself back?

Sorrow and compassion filled him. He ached to ease that pain from her.

He couldn't let her back into his life. She'd chosen her path. But he could do everything in his power to see that she returned to her Wallmer Grove physically unharmed, even if he couldn't heal either of their wounds.

In the end, it was decided that Katie would stay overnight at the bishop's *haus*. She surprised him by not arguing when the bishop declared it was too late for her to go to the B&B.

Uneasy at leaving her, he departed and returned home.

The next morning, Kate was standing outside, enjoying the sunshine on her face when she heard Abram's voice in the house. She smiled, then mentally chastised herself for being happy that he had arrived. The smile fell from her face when the space between her shoulder blades had tightened.

Something didn't feel right.

Kate set the basket she was holding against her left hip and casually rotated, scanning the area around her as nonchalantly as she could. When breakfast was finished, she'd offered to put the first load on the clothesline for Edith while she cleaned up. It was an excuse. She'd wanted to be helpful, yes, but she also needed to escape the closed-in atmosphere of the house. Sitting at a table with the bishop and her childhood best friend had had her grinding her teeth.

No one had been mean, or offensive. Still, the memories had nearly suffocated her. The bishop and Edith had both tried to convince her to stay with them instead of the bed-and-breakfast. Kate stood her ground. She appreciated the offer but would go to the bed-and-breakfast as planned. Standing outside in the September sun had settled her. She'd closed her eyes and breathed in the sweet air, lightly scented with woodsmoke. Someone was burning leaves nearby.

Until her shoulders had prickled. Was someone watching her? Her mouth went dry. She shouldn't have come. While she hated disappointing Captain Murphy, perhaps coming here was a mistake. Between the people she'd hurt and the memories she'd escaped, she wasn't the best option for this mission, even if she did know the people and the culture.

"Bist du gut?"

Abram.

If someone were out here with a gun, she didn't want an unarmed civilian here. Of course, her own weapon would be a little awkward to get to. She'd grabbed the apron Captain Murphy had provided. There was a pocket sewn into the back of the apron for her weapon. She had actually felt guilty for putting her gun in it. The Amish in her old community didn't have pockets in their clothing. She cringed when she turned too fast and the weight of the weapon thumped against her stomach.

None of that mattered. If necessary, she'd use the gun in a heartbeat to protect those around her.

She hoped she wouldn't have to. Wallmer Grove wasn't that large. The crime in the area was mostly minor infractions. Since she'd joined the Wallmer

Grove Police Department, she'd never even had to fire her gun except during drills and on the range.

"I'm fine," she answered him in a near whisper. "I feel like I'm being watched, though."

His face hardened. He turned away. She knew he was planning on going after whoever it was. Without thinking, she grabbed his arm, letting the basket slide to the ground.

He halted, amazed. His gaze shot to her hand holding his arm, then back to her face.

Backing up like she'd been burned, her face flushed. But she wouldn't back down. "Think, Abram. He probably has a knife or a gun, if anyone's there. What would you do?"

"I would give you time to escape."

Her mouth fell open and she gaped at him. He'd risk his life so she could escape. Had he always been so noble? If only he'd been with her that day...

She shook her head. "Abram. I'm the one with a gun hidden in my apron."

His face froze. "You have a gun?"

"Yeah." She picked up the basket and moved toward the house, her eyes still scanning. "I'm a cop, remember?"

She saw the glint of sunlight striking steel.

"Get down!"

A gunshot cracked through the quiet. The taut clothesline snapped as the bullet ripped through it.

She didn't know how it happened. One moment they were standing side by side, and the next Abram had pushed her down and was protecting her with his own body. She pushed slightly. Abram moved back, still hovering, ready to push her back again if another bullet came flying toward them.

"Into the house," she whispered.

Abram pulled her to her feet and they both ran through the door. A second bullet smashed into the side of the house.

Kate pulled her phone from the pocket sewn into her apron. She had Marshal Delacure on speed dial, thanks to Captain Murphy's overzealous need to be organized. Abram rushed into the other room. She heard him ushering the bishop and Edith into the bishop's office. If she recalled, there were no windows in that room. It was a good choice.

"The marshals are on their way," she told Abram when he dashed into the room.

He bobbed his head in acknowledgment. "*Gut*. You weren't injured?"

Her heart melted the teeniest bit before she shoved the emotions aside. His putting himself between her and the sniper wasn't sweet. He could have been hurt. Or killed. After all, she was the one in law enforcement.

Thinking of him being injured, she felt like a giant fist had reached inside her chest and was squeezing her heart. She pressed the heel of her hand to her chest to ease the ache.

"I'm fine. What were you thinking?"

He didn't bat an eye. "I was thinking someone was shooting at us."

She huffed. Going to the door, she looked out. She couldn't see anyone. Which meant nothing. The sniper could have moved or hunkered down. Until she saw the flash of the sun's rays reflecting off the gun, she hadn't known where he was before. All she'd known was that someone was watching her.

Smirking, Abram left for a moment when the bishop called out to him.

She remembered what the man who'd tried to abduct her looked like. It wasn't a face she was likely to ever forget.

She frowned. She still had her phone. Could she gain access to the criminal database and search for him, maybe give them a place to start?

Abram stalked back into the room. He speared her with a fierce stare. He was chomping on a piece of gum. Probably a stress reliever for him. "The bishop and his wife are safe. You aren't, though."

"I will be once he's caught," she said, evading his gaze. "I can't leave, though. Beth is still out there. I don't care how suspicious her disappearance is. I think she's in trouble."

He took two more steps in her direction, bringing him close enough for her to smell the mint gum he'd been chewing. It was a scent she'd remembered well from their times together years ago.

The sudden yearning for all that she'd lost swamped her. In all the years since she'd left, she'd steered clear of emotional entanglements, except for Shane and his wife. But that was different. He was married and treated her like a kid sister.

She'd tried dating exactly three times. Whenever her date had tried to kiss her, she bolted.

Never had she dreamed of wanting more than she had as a cop. Because while her life was solitary and often empty, it was still safer than letting someone tromp all over her heart or stealing the joy from her soul.

Funny thing was, she hadn't had much joy, either. Not since she left Abram and tossed God out of her life. He hadn't protected her when she was at her most vulnerable. It was hard to trust that He would help her now.

A car pulled into the drive.

"The marshals are here." Abram went to the trash can to dispose of his gum. "Hopefully, they'll find this guy and you'll be able to concentrate on finding Beth."

She moved to the door to greet them without responding. All these strange emotions swirling through her left her unsettled. It would only get worse if she stayed. She was right. She wasn't the person Beth needed.

A quick glance showed her that Abram was right behind her. Her pulse skipped when his breath washed across her cheek, ruffling the tendrils that had escaped her *kapp* and laid over her ear. She shivered.

She needed to leave soon before she got in over her head.

If it wasn't already too late.

SIX

Kate itched to join in the search as the marshals combed through the woods. She was tasked with staying on patrol at the house to make sure no harm came to the bishop or his wife. Scowling, she gazed after the marshals. They'd tagged Lieutenant Greer on the call, which surprised her. She hadn't thought they were that keen on sharing the case. An active shooting, however, took precedent over a jurisdiction squabble.

"Is your job normally this exciting?" Abram squinted as he stared toward the sun in the direction the marshals had gone.

She scoffed. "Not really. I do take special pride in putting away criminals, especially those who have harmed children. But there's a lot of paperwork in my job. Lots of small petty crimes, too. Honestly, I think I spend more time behind my desk than on the streets."

"Why'd you leave here?"

His question slammed into her, stealing her breath. She should have been expecting it. If she'd been in his shoes, she would have asked him before he'd even said hello. Really, he'd been extraordinarily patient.

Regardless, she wasn't ready to answer. Not yet.

Maybe not ever. She opened her mouth. Closed it, then tried again. Nothing. She had nothing to give him, no excuse, because she couldn't lie to him. "I can't tell you yet."

She winced. Yet, made it sound like she'd tell him someday. But how could she? She'd borne her parents' disgust before their deaths. She didn't think she could handle Abram's.

Abram nodded like he'd expected that reply. "*Ja.* Now isn't a *gut* time, with the marshals and the bishop and Edith here. I can wait."

The words twisted inside her like a blade, slicing deeper into her already-shredded heart.

Lieutenant Greer jogged toward them, his face set.

"You didn't find anything," Katie commented.

"Well." The lieutenant halted before them. "Yes and no. We didn't find a trace here, but if it's the guy from the hospital, we have an ID."

Her heart thumped and adrenaline shot through her. "Who?"

He pulled out his phone and showed her a picture.

"Yes." She jabbed her finger at the familiar face glaring out at her. "That's the man who grabbed me."

Lieutenant Greer pocketed the phone again. "His name is Evan Stiles. He was a local college student busted last year for dealing drugs as well as assault. Some believe he had ties to a local drug ring that was broken up a few years ago."

"I know about that one," Abram interjected. "My brother Levi got caught up in that when they went after Lilah, his wife. This was before they were married. I thought the ring was finished. The leader and several of his underlings were arrested."

"Yep. Same crime ring. It was bad. Drugs, possibly even some ties to human trafficking. No proof, though. I've had my doubts that the ring was truly gone. Looks like they might have a new leader."

"Hold on." Kate left the men when Marshal Delacure motioned her over.

"He got away," the marshal said, "but we know who he is. I really need you to dig deep and find any clues about what happened to Beth. How was she connected with all this?"

She had to say something now. Her emotions were too close to the surface. What if they caused her to make a mistake? She was no longer confident in her ability to compartmentalize them. "Actually, Marshal, I'm wondering if I'm the right person for the job, now that someone is after me."

The marshal shook her head. "No. I actually think you're still the best person. I meant what I told Tim. You grew up here. These people will be more willing to talk with you than someone like me. Your connection could be our only chance of finding Beth. Especially when people see you with Abram. He's a respected member of the community. I talked with the bishop earlier. His brother is an elder of some kind. No, you are the best choice. I'm convinced that the time it takes to find someone else and make inroads would come at the cost of Beth's life. Our only hope of getting her back alive is using the advantage you bring."

She couldn't say no. Even if staying resulted in her shattered heart. Surely, saving the other woman's life was worth more than her own private pain?

Nodding, she turned from the marshal and returned to Abram's side. He was frowning as he scanned the sky.

"Something wrong?" Tipping her head back, she sighed as she saw the dark clouds rolling in. She'd forgotten that rain was on the horizon.

"I think we're going to be driving into a storm." Abram shrugged. "We can't do anything about it."

Less than an hour later, Abram had the buggy hooked up and was waiting for her so they could go to the bed-and-breakfast. The sun was completely hidden behind the dark cover of clouds. Kate shivered as the wind picked up. The temperature was dropping, too.

The bishop and Edith had urged her to stay with them, but she wouldn't budge. Her being there had already brought violence to their home.

Hugging Edith, she swallowed the lump in her throat and turned away, hopping up on the bench of the buggy. Too late, she realized she should have ducked inside. The buggy was turning onto the road.

Awkward. That described her current situation, sitting next to Abram. It didn't feel like it was ten years ago since they'd been planning their first date. They both acted like they didn't have a history. Except they did, and it was stealing her focus.

Two minutes into the drive, the wind picked up and a cold rain fell. The icy drops were spitting in her face. She shivered, crossing her arms over her chest. She cast a glance at the overcast sky. It was growing darker by the second. Great.

"There's a blanket behind the seat." Abram's voice broke into her thoughts of gloom and doom.

"Oh, thanks." She reached behind and grabbed one, pulling it around her shoulders. When it snagged on his toolbox sitting behind the seat, he released the reins with his right hand. His fingers grazed her arm when he reached back, unsnagged the blanket and handed it to her. Her cheeks flared red. Her breath hitched in her throat.

This needed to stop. Maybe if she concentrated on her case.

"Tell me about Beth," she said to him.

"Shouldn't you already know about her?"

She turned to scan his face for any sign of snarkiness. When their eyes met, all she saw was remote curiosity. It was, she supposed, a fair question. "You'd think, right? But no, the marshals gave me very little information about her. Only that she lived here and worked at the B&B."

"You said you'd met her."

So he'd been paying attention at the hospital.

"I met her once, several years ago. She was battered and nearly half dead after her crime boss ex-boyfriend tried to kill her. She had information that could, and did, put him in jail. Hopefully for the rest of his life."

"She was attacked?"

She glanced at him, catching an odd note in his voice. Maybe it was an illusion, but he appeared to be a shade paler. Her belly clenched. She'd wondered how he'd react. Was he blaming Beth for what had happened to her?

She'd made the correct choice not to tell him about Gary the Shark. It had been hard enough dealing with her mother's lamentations and disgust. His rejection would have killed her.

She locked up those thoughts. They served no purpose.

"When did Beth disappear?"

"No one knows exactly," he said and maneuvered the horse to turn right. "She had a weekend off. It was a visiting weekend, so no one noticed if she was gone or not. The next day, she was supposed to work. She never showed up. When my *onkel* went to her *haus*, there was no answer. He went back and checked again two days before you arrived."

"Wait. Did he go to the back door?"

He gave her a strange glance. "*Ja.* We always use that door. You know that. Most of the Amish around here only use the front door for visitors."

She waved that aside. "I know. This is important, Abram. When my partner and I went there yesterday, we went to the back door, but the door was open."

His head reared back, shocked. "*Nee*, it was closed when my *onkel* checked on her. I'm sure of it."

"So, someone has been in and out of the house since she's been gone. The bishop and your *onkel* have both been out there, and neither of them were caught in an explosion nor noticed the open door. So that means whoever was there went after your *onkel* had left, within forty-eight hours of my arrival. That was when the bomb was put in place."

Was the bomb for Beth? Had someone wanted her dead? Or had Beth planted the bomb? It was hard picturing the former socialite making an explosive. However, the blast hadn't been effective. Possibly because an amateur made it. Whatever had happened, she needed to begin her investigation. Anyone willing to rig a bomb had to have a reason.

The wind had picked up by the time they arrived at the bed-and-breakfast. Kate tugged the black bonnet she wore over her *kapp* closer to her face to avoid getting hit in the face with flying dust or debris. She flicked her gaze over the bed-and-breakfast. It was a large, sturdy structure, built to resemble an oversize barn. They walked under a hanging awning to get to the front door. She didn't remember Abram's relatives owning a bed-and-breakfast ten years ago. It was probably a relatively new business. Of course, her *daed* would have frowned upon it. He was uncomfortable living so close to the *Englisch*.

Abram opened the door for her and followed her inside. For a second, she was tempted to tell him she was fine and he could go. It would be a waste of breath. Abram had always done what he wanted. Ridiculously, the thought cheered her somewhat.

She nodded her thanks and preceded him inside the building. It was cheerful and bright. And dry. A sigh of pleasure escaped before she could contain it. Moving to the counter, she introduced herself. The young Amish girl's eyes widened slightly. She glanced at Abram quickly before she smiled and checked her in, making polite conversation. She was a cute little thing with big brown eyes and dark hair peeping out from under the *kapp*. When Abram stepped up to the counter, her smile widened and warmed. Kate fought back a hot wave of jealousy. She had no right to feel that way.

Kate thanked the girl behind the check-in counter and gathered her key. Did the girl think it was strange to have someone dressed Plain staying at the bed-and-breakfast instead of in a relative's home?

Turning away from the reception desk, she walked toward the stairs.

Abram waved at the girl. "Later, Adele."

"*Ja*. Tell *Aenti* Fanny that *Mamm* enjoyed the pie she made."

"Will do."

The jealousy drained. She was an idiot. She'd not even recognized Abram's younger cousin, Adele. No wonder the girl had looked at her. Did Adele know about her relationship with Abram? She'd have to apologize later for not greeting her.

As she walked toward the hall, the front door opened, letting in a blast of wind.

"Hi, Adele. Where do you want these?"

That voice. The chill that shuddered through her had nothing to do with the cold. Dodging into the open door of the library, Kate huddled against the wall, a prisoner of her own terror as memories recalled by that voice pelted her. She squeezed her eyes shut and covered her ears, begging them to stop.

She no longer knew, or cared, where she was or who was with her.

All her terrified mind could comprehend at the moment was that the man she called Gary the Shark was here.

Abram had no idea what had happened. One minute, Katie was stalking toward the stairs as if she were on a mission, and then in the space of two heartbeats, she was huddled down against the wall. Her face was colorless. Squatting down, he stared into her huge haunted blue eyes. His mouth went dry. The terror etched on her face was the scariest thing he'd ever seen in his life.

Did she even know he was there?

He called her name, softly.

After the third time, she turned his way, her hands reaching out, feeling the air in front of her as if she'd gone blind. What had happened to her?

"Abram!" Her voice was a harsh whisper. She choked on the rest of her words.

"Shush. Katie, I'm here."

Please, Gott, let me help her. In that instant, he dropped the bitterness he'd been carrying around like a shield. The Katie he'd known had been fearless and indomitable. This woman was terrified beyond reason.

A deep male laugh rolled through the establishment. Katie's hands clenched around his. She shuddered so hard her head hit the wall behind her.

It was him. The man talking to his cousin. Something about that man scared her half to death. He had to get Katie out of there. But he couldn't leave his cousin with a man who had this effect on his former love. However horrible Katie's connection with him was, the scars went deep.

A door opened at the other end of the hall. Abram patted Katie's shoulder and stepped out. His *onkel* smiled a greeting and started to move past. Abram put out a hand to halt him.

"One moment, *Onkel Dean*." He hesitated. He didn't know what had happened with Katie and Gary. The less he said about that until he knew more, the better. "That guy who does the deliveries? I don't like the way he's flirting with Adele. He gives me a bad feeling."

In his periphery, Katie cringed.

Onkel Dean's mouth firmed. "*Ja.* I've seen him flirt with her before. I'll watch her. And him."

Once his *onkel* was passed, Abram helped Katie to her feet and guided her toward the kitchen. "We'll sit on the porch and talk, *ja?*"

She nodded, her face drawn and exhausted. The

defiance she'd worn like a cloak had slipped from her shoulders. He missed the spark in her eyes.

The porch was screened in, protecting them from the deluge outside. "The guests like to see the outdoors without dealing with the weather."

She nodded and sat at the table. "Gary used to make deliveries to my *daed*'s shop, too."

He blinked, astonished that she'd volunteered any information so quick. He didn't want to drag it out. Nor did he want to force her to tell details that would leave her feeling vulnerable. "He hurt you, didn't he?"

She blanched. He exclaimed and shot to his feet as the little color that had returned to her cheeks bled away. When he touched her cold hands, she snatched them from his grasp and hid them in her apron.

"Katie." Shock mingled with hurt reverberated through him. She was scared of him. Didn't she know he'd never hurt her?

It wasn't him. He knew that. He'd seen the effects of an attack before. His heart darkened. *Ja*, he'd seen this kind of reaction before. His cousin Marta, though, had recovered, thanks to her faith and the love of her family. They were overjoyed when she'd met her husband and moved on.

"I'll never hurt you, you know that, ain't so?"

Her lips pressed together. Not in defiance. A tear streamed from her eyes. No, she was broken.

Suddenly, her eyes flashed and she straightened in her chair. "Enough. I'm a grown woman and a cop. He can't hurt me."

"Did you go to the *Englisch* police?" He lowered himself back down beside her, holding his breath until it was clear she wouldn't flinch away from him. He didn't need to hear any more details of what had happened.

"How?" Half turning in her seat, her eyes met his. Her facade of calm was back in place, but now that he knew what to look for, he could easily spot the soul-deep woundedness in her gaze. "My parents wouldn't let me."

"I know we don't usually go to the police, but in this instance—"

"They were ashamed of me. I think they blamed me for letting it happen."

That knocked the breath out of him. "You? Katie, you were sixteen. How could you be responsible?" Now her reaction when he'd said no one could be held responsible for another's actions made sense.

She shrugged. "I don't know. All I know is that the last few months I lived here were impossible. And then they were gone, and I realized there was nothing holding me here."

"*Ja*, there was. Or there should have been."

There had been him.

Her mouth worked like she were trying to chew something really tough. "I would have stayed for you but, Abram, after the way *Mamm* and *Daed* reacted, I no longer knew how you'd react." She averted her gaze. "Nor did I have faith to comfort me."

Whoa. He hadn't expected that. Hadn't known Gary had destroyed that part of her. How did one survive without faith? He needed to step gently. "When my brother Levi was in Afghanistan and lost his arm while saving a friend, he let his faith go for a few years."

"Levi was a soldier? I knew he'd left, but I never realized…"

"He left the Amish and became *Englisch* for a few years. He's back now. He's a deacon."

Her eyes flared wide open. "I know that Marshal Delacure said you had a brother who was an elder of some kind. I didn't connect it with Levi."

"Well, he found his faith, so maybe you could, too. *Gott* didn't abandon Levi when he was going through the darkest time in his life. Nor did He abandon you." Katie wasn't convinced; he could see that. If only he could find a way to wedge open her closed-up heart and help her believe again.

She frowned. "Maybe not. But I abandoned Him. I don't even know if I could go back now."

"You can always go back." He cleared his throat and lowered his voice. "I wouldn't have blamed you. My cousin went through something similar. I saw how devastated she was. She never told anyone who had hurt her until the one responsible was killed in a farming accident."

She teared up, but didn't say anything.

He continued, "If you want to go to the police now, I'll go with you."

She half snorted, half snickered. "Abram, I am the police."

Oh. He'd almost forgotten that.

She sighed. "Even if I wanted to, it's too late. This was ten years ago. If I had evidence that he was still doing things like that…"

Suddenly, she jumped up.

"What?"

"Abram!" She whirled and grabbed his forearms. "Didn't Lieutenant Greer say that the crime ring might have had ties to human trafficking?"

"*Ja*, I think he did."

"I remember hearing Gary on the phone, before the attack, talking about a buyer and a seller. His face was scary mad. What if he hadn't been talking about his normal supplies? What if he was connected to the human-trafficking league back then and still is?"

Immediately, he understood.

"You think that he's behind the disappearance of Beth."

Katie paced the length of the porch and back. "We have no evidence. No proof. But the man is certainly on my suspect list."

"How does he know the man who tried to kidnap you?"

"Well, if they are both involved in the same ring, that would be enough, right? My guess is they have no clue that I'm a cop. Even if they saw us today, I didn't help with the search. I was steamed about it then, but in retrospect, it was a good call. No, I think that something happened, and they think that Beth and I were in league together."

She fascinated him. The way her mind worked. "What do they think you two know, or did? That's the important thing, *ja*?"

"*Ja.*" She shook her head. "I mean, yes."

He grinned at her slip back into Pennsylvania Dutch. "I think it's time you called Marshal Delacure again and set up a meeting."

She turned and smiled at him. The light blazing in

her eyes burrowed inside his chest. He wondered if he'd ever truly be free of her now.

"You're absolutely right," she told him. "We need to make a plan. One way or another, Gary and this crime ring needs to end."

SEVEN

Even as excited as she was about this possible new lead, Kate still didn't want to go back inside. Coming face-to-face with Gary was not on her bucket list. If she'd never heard his voice or seen him again, she wouldn't have complained.

Except now she had the opportunity to see that he answered for his crimes. Spinning it around in her brain, it seemed likely that he had committed many crimes, not only against her. If he were the leader of the new crime ring, she needed to see him brought to justice.

A sudden urge took her by storm. Pivoting on her heel, she crossed the porch to Abram in three steps, bringing her close enough to feel the warmth of his breath on her face. His eyes widened a bit, but he didn't back away.

"Abram." She kept her voice low, unsure how to ask what she wanted. "I want to pray."

The awe dawning on his face made her shift her gaze away. Her cheeks warmed. Doubtless, she was the color of a ripe tomato about now.

"*Ja*, that's a *gut* thing to do when you're in trouble."

Puffing her cheeks, she blew out a calming breath. "Yeah. The thing is, it's been so long, I'm not sure how to begin."

His finger grazed her cheek, leaving a tingling path in its wake. "Katie, would you like me to pray for you?"

She nodded, unable to speak around the emotion clogging her throat.

He bowed his head. Their foreheads touched, but neither backed away.

"Dear *Gott*, we ask for Your protection and guidance. Show us the right way to go. Keep Katie safe, and help her heal. Let us bring Beth home. Amen."

She nodded and stepped back, clearing her throat. "Thanks."

The simple prayer touched her.

"Let's go."

Striding back inside the building, she saw that Adele was again by herself at the reception desk. Breathing easier, Kate ran up to her room and dropped her bag off. She pressed her apron, the familiar presence of her weapon steadying her. She had a job to do and people to serve. Pulling out her phone, she called Marshal Delacure.

"I'm at my hotel in town," Amy Delacure told her. "Why don't you join me here and we'll get all our ducks in a row."

After agreeing, Kate ended the call. Her phone would need to be charged soon. She didn't have time now, but the moment she returned she'd be sure to plug it in. Slipping it back into the pocket hidden in her apron, she checked her appearance in the mirror. Something plinked against the windowpane. Walking over, she looked out and groaned. Mixed in with the rain were bits of ice. Hail. Sighing, she grabbed her bag and tugged out the light cloak and then exited her room. Closing her door, she returned downstairs to join Abram.

"She said to meet her at her hotel," she told him. He merely nodded and held the front door open for her. Always the gentleman, she smiled at him.

"What?"

"Nothing." She ducked her head and quickened her step, remonstrating her foolish heart for getting soft where he was concerned. It didn't matter how kind or brave he was. No matter how far he went to help her, the truth that stood between them would never change. Abram Burkholder was a baptized member of the Amish church, whereas she barely even knew what she believed anymore. One prayer in a desperate moment didn't change the fact that she spent nearly a decade of her life willfully trying to ignore God or His existence. She wasn't even sure where one went from there.

A huge drop of ice bouncing off her nose brought her attention back to the moment.

"Yuck." She wiped her nose. It hadn't hurt, but the cold wetness on her nose was irritating.

Abram laughed. It nearly stopped her in her tracks. That gorgeous rolling laugh that had always made her want to laugh along, even when she didn't know what he was laughing at. She hadn't heard it in so long. The wound in her soul ached.

She'd missed that sound in her life.

"Let's not stand out here in the open," Abram murmured. "I know you can look after yourself, Katie, but I don't care to take any chances."

Scanning the area for danger, she strode to where the buggy was still parked. She reached out a hand to open the door so she could climb inside the black buggy. That would be the smart thing to do. Instead, she pulled herself up onto the front seat and yanked her cloak closer around her neck and arms. It wasn't much protection against the rain, but she couldn't make herself move to the back.

When he sat down next to her, the faint sway of the buggy caused her to lurch to the side. Their arms brushed. She pulled back, but the tingling running up and down her arm was as bad as sticking a bobby pin into an electrical socket. Absently, she rubbed her opposite hand up and down her arm, stopping when she caught Abram peeking out the corner of his eye at her, a smirk tugging at the corner of his mouth. Had he felt it, too?

She clasped her hands together in her lap, trying to pretend that the attraction between them wasn't a distraction from her duty.

Duty. That's what she needed to focus on. The sooner they found Beth and locked Gary away, the sooner her life could resume. Funny how unappealing that was.

A vibration against her hip startled her. Reaching under her apron, she fetched her phone and looked at the number.

"It's Marshal Delacure." She unlocked the device and accepted the call. "Hey, Marshal. Where're on our way."

"Okay, listen, I got called out for a few minutes and am actually not too far from the B&B. Is there somewhere else you want to meet?"

"Let me ask Abram." She removed the phone from her ear, then screamed as the buggy lurched awkwardly.

A sharp snap came from in front of them.

"What was that?" she yelled at Abram.

His knuckles on the reins were white. "The bridle's breaking."

Sure enough, one of the leather straps on the right side of the bridle had broken. She's never seen that happen before. Abram had always taken excellent care of his tack. He'd never allow it to get worn enough to break naturally.

He tried to rein the horse in. The uneven reins, though, confused the horse. Instead of slowing, the beast trotted at an angle. Kate screamed as he barely managed to steer the horse out of the path of an on-coming pickup truck. The driver honked and yelled rudely out his window.

The buggy lurched again. The cell phone clenched in her fist flew out of her hand and soared through the opening in the front of the buggy; it crashed onto the road, shattering.

Abram sucked in a harsh breath.

Whipping her face to the front, her heart slammed in her chest. They were nearing a curve in the road. The buggy was weaving, picking up speed as the road started to slant down. Looking beyond the curve, she saw the lake sprawling out like a great yawning pit.

"Abram." Her throat was dry, making it hard to get the word out.

"Ja!" He didn't remove his gaze from the horse or the road.

"I can't swim."

Her fingers ached from gripping the edge of the

bench to hold herself steady. Prayers she hadn't thought herself capable of uttering rose to her mind in a litany of desperate pleas.

Maybe they'd make it. If he could control the horse long enough.

The curve loomed ahead. The horse started to swerve. A hard snap ripped through the air. Untethered, the horse continued on. The buggy, in the grip of inertia and the downward slope of the land, continued sailing forward. They flew over the berm and crashed through the shallow wooden guardrail.

She screamed as the buggy caved in, trapping her legs like a safety bar on a roller coaster. The box flipped and tumbled, hitting the water roof first.

Her scream cut off as the front of the buggy dipped below the water and the bitter cold liquid gushed into her mouth. She struggled to move, but was trapped.

Abram held his breath and kicked himself free of the wrecked buggy. Turning back, his heart nearly stopped beating in his chest. Katie was so still. Her legs were wedged under the crumpled metal. Reaching in, he took hold of her arms and tugged. Her torso moved in his direction, then stopped. Her apron was caught on a shard of broken buggy. Grabbing it in his hands, he yanked until the white fabric was torn and he could pull her free. It took some maneuvering, but he managed to shift her so her legs slid free.

His lungs burned with the need for oxygen. He had to hold on for a few more seconds. He seized Kate's too-still form and pulled her out of the car and brought her head above the surface of the cold water.

The lake wasn't that deep. It was only a few strokes

before his feet found purchase on the sand beneath the water. They'd been under less than two minutes, but cars were stopped all along the berm. A siren wailing in the distance alerted him that help was approaching, fast.

It might be too late.

Staggering to the soggy grass, he placed his burden down and dropped to his knees beside her, heedless of the mud or the gapers surrounding him. He only had room in his mind for Katie.

She wasn't breathing.

Come on, Katie. Breathe. You can do it.

Nothing. Her lips and skin had a blueish tint, which sent horror coursing through his veins. What had Levi said? Chest compressions. And rescue breaths. He recalled Levi saying rescue breaths weren't taught anymore due to possible contagion.

He didn't care.

Plugging her nose with his fingers and tilting her chin, Abram covered her mouth with his and blew. Her chest rose. He blew again, giving her life-saving oxygen.

Swiftly rising, he wiped the wetness from his cheek and blinked, then moved into position and began chest compressions.

Someone landed across from him. Marshal Delacure. He ignored her.

"Breathe, Katie. Breathe. You're too stubborn to die."

She gasped and choked, her eyes popping open. Marshal Delacure grabbed her by the hip and shoulder and turned her on her side. Katie sobbed as she expelled the water she'd swallowed.

Abram wilted back on the grass. Bracing his arm

on his knee, he covered his face with his hands. He didn't realize he was crying until Marshal Delacure stood beside him rubbing his shoulder.

"She'll be fine. The ambulance is pulling in now. You saved her."

Wiping his eyes clear with his thumb and forefinger, he nodded at her. "*Ja*. She'll live. *Gott* is *gut*."

"Yeah. Well, she's fortunate you were with her when the accident happened."

"Accident?" His head snapped up. "That was no accident. Bridles don't snap like that. Especially not bridles less than a month old. Those were cut on purpose."

"When would they have been cut?" Her gaze bore into his.

"At the bed-and-breakfast." Kate's raw voice broke through before she was racked with a coughing fit.

The paramedics were climbing out of the ambulance. A second emergency vehicle, a long red-and-white truck with a box-shaped trailer, pulled alongside the ambulance. Scuba Team was painted on the side. A tall lanky woman in her early thirties jumped out and followed the ambulance crew. The other door opened, and a shorter male joined her.

"Any bodies in the water?" the man demanded.

The woman winced but kept her smile in place. She appeared embarrassed by her partner. Abram aimed his reply to her.

"It was only us," he informed her.

"Natasha," one of the paramedics called to her.

"Excuse me." Natasha moved away.

Abram was forced aside as the medical professionals swarmed around Katie.

"I don't want to go to the hospital." Her hoarse voice

was barely audible over the noise. Still, he heard it and moved closer.

"Ma'am," one of them patiently explained. "You swallowed water and needed CPR. We need to check you out. It's possible the CPR broke your ribs. We have to make sure you're okay."

"Go with them, Katie," Abram said, insinuating himself into the conversation. "Please. Marshal Delacure and I will meet you there. When you're done, I'll drive you out to my *haus* this afternoon. You can stay and have supper with my family. We can talk there."

The militant light in her gaze told him she had no intention of going to his family home. Whether it was to protect them or to keep some sort of distance between them, he had no idea. Katie was stubborn. *Ack.* She could be more stubborn than anyone he'd ever met. Well, this time, she'd have to deal with him being even more stubborn. He wouldn't leave her by herself at the bed-and-breakfast when someone was out to get her. Someone who could have been Gary, or maybe was someone totally unrelated.

Katie's chin wobbled. He stared her down, even though his heart broke for her. He knew she was scared and scarred. He also suspected she'd been pretending to be brave for so long she didn't know how to stop pretending.

Unexpectedly, she relented and allowed herself to be loaded onto a stretcher. Too weary to argue, no doubt.

The paramedics lifted the stretcher and moved her through the throng of onlookers.

"Abram!" Her panicked voice rose above the crowd. He was at the back of the ambulance in two steps.

"I'm here, Katie. We'll be directly behind you. We won't be far."

There was nothing else he could do for her.

The helpless feeling gnawing into his chest wasn't one he was used to.

"Come on. We'll be there when she gets done being examined by the doctor," Marshal Delacure said, standing beside him, her quiet voice filled with understanding.

"Ja."

He nearly tripped over the edge of the road, his attention was focused on the ambulance pulling away and driving toward Berlin. How he made it to the car in one piece, he wasn't quite sure. He bit back the temptation to urge Marshal Delacure to drive faster.

She was a good driver. And her car was faster than a buggy would have been, that was certain. However, when she stopped at a red light, he was still impatient, and somewhat anxious, as the woman who'd done nothing but disturb his peace of mind since she'd crashed back into his life moved farther and farther away until the ambulance wasn't even a speck in the distance.

After what was possibly the longest red light in the Midwest, the light changed. The marshal's car moved smoothly forward. He gritted his teeth. She was being safe.

"I'm going as fast as I can," she told him, glancing pointedly at his left leg, vibrating with the force of his impatience.

"Sorry. I don't want her to arrive and we're not there."

"I get that. They're going to rush her into the emergency room. She won't know we're not there. Besides, we'll be there long before the doctors have finished."

He'd have to be satisfied with that, despite the desperation crawling up his spine. He needed to know she'd be fine. He had never been so scared as the moment he saw she wasn't breathing. He'd have nightmares for years.

She was alive. She was breathing and talking. And arguing. Surely, he didn't need to worry about that anymore.

He wrenched his mind back to the matter of the snipped bridle. It had to have happened when they were talking about Gary. Could the man have seen Katie and recognized her? Was he afraid she'd make trouble for him?

When the car finally parked in the lot, Abram shot from the car and strode toward the emergency room doors.

"Easy, Abram. We're here."

"*Ja*. As soon as she's out and ready to go, we need to leave. There are things you need to know to keep Katie safe. Maybe they will help you find Beth and solve this whole case. But not here. We need to go back to my parents' *haus*."

Her mouth dropped open. She snapped it shut. "The bed-and-breakfast—"

"Is no longer safe."

She was obviously burning with questions. So was he. But the most important thing on his mind right now was seeing Katie and making sure she survived. The only way he could ensure that was if he never let her out of his sight.

Knowing how stubborn and independent she was, that would take some work on his part. He would do whatever he needed to, however, to see that she was safe and whole when she returned to Wallmer Grove. He, on the other hand, didn't know if he'd ever be completely free ever again.

EIGHT

Searing pain brought her out of the light sleep she'd fallen into waiting for the emergency room doctor to come and examine her. Her chest hurt and her lungs were on fire. Breathing hurt. So much. At the same time, she welcomed every agonizing breath, recalling those moments when water filled her lungs. She had been sure she was a goner.

Who would have missed her?

Kate had no family, not anymore. Her parents were gone, and it had been years since she'd had any communication with her sisters. She wasn't even sure where they were anymore. Her brother, her only other sibling, had been dead for years. There was no one left.

She had friends, like Shane. But he had his own wife and family. No, the sad truth was that no one would miss her. Not really.

Abram? Her eyelids fluttered open at the idea. Would Abram miss her? She cringed back against the pillow. She didn't want him to bear the burden of missing her. But she would miss him.

A hand grabbed the curtain and slid it open. The doctor stepped inside the cubicle, a surgical mask covering the entire bottom portion of his face. He was wearing blue scrubs.

Something was off. She frowned. The man before her approached the bed silently. Her gaze slid to his hands. They were empty. Shouldn't he at least have a clipboard? Despite the pain, she pushed herself to a sitting position. Her dress was mostly dry. Her feet were bare.

Shifting closer to the edge of the bed, she eyed the large man coming closer. Wisps of a dark beard wrapped around the edges of the mask. Those eyes— she'd seen them before.

Right before he'd tried to kidnap her from the hospital the first time.

Kate opened her mouth to scream. The weak sound that emerged from her throat was cut off when the mountain of a man lunged at her, his large hands closing in around her throat. Grabbing his thick wrists, she yanked. He didn't budge.

"Uh-uh. You got away from me once. Made me look like an idiot in front of the boss. That's not going to happen again. I'm going to take care of you so you can't tell any tales."

She had no idea what tales he thought she'd tell, and she wasn't in any position to ask.

Kate wouldn't go down without a fight. When she was sixteen, she'd been the victim. She was a strong woman now, and she would fight for her life.

Her bare foot kicked out, slamming into his knee. Caught off guard, he stumbled, bellowing in pain. His hands slipped off her throat.

Sucking in a breath, she screamed as hard and loud

as she could, despite the agony ripping through her. Would it be enough?

"Help! He's trying to kill me!" She collapsed in a fit of coughing on the bed. If he came at her again, she'd be too weak to fight him off.

With a growl, the man stumbled out of the cubicle, tripping over the tray at the end of her bed. It toppled to the ground with a bang. Feet pounded in the corridor. Shouts were lifted as her assailant fled, knocking two nurses down before he was out of her sight.

Abram and Marshal Delacure ran into the cubicle. Seeing she was alive, the marshal took off in the direction the bearded man had gone.

Abram rushed to her side and gathered Kate into his strong arms. She melted against him, letting him comfort her. His heart raced against her ear. Snuggling in closer, she closed her eyes and shut out everything but him.

As his heart rate slowed, strength returned to her weary muscles. She backed away.

"Katie, did he hurt you?" Abram gently touched her neck where brutal hands had been clamped moments before. She could only guess how red her skin was. By tomorrow, she'd be sporting a few bruises.

But she was alive.

A question stirred in her soul. Had God orchestrated her rescue? Abram and the marshal had arrived in the nick of time. God hadn't saved her before. She'd never fully understood why He allowed His children to suffer.

Brisk footsteps outside the cubicle announced Marshal Delacure returning. A harried doctor was on her heels.

"Sorry, Miss Bontrager. I can't tell you how awful I feel that you were attacked in our hospital!"

Apparently, the doctor hadn't been brought up to speed on the events of the past day. Well, she didn't have the patience to enlighten him. Urgency coursed through her veins.

She waved the apology away. "I need to get out of here."

There was no way she'd stick around this place any longer than necessary. She'd been nearly kidnapped and murdered in this hospital. Who knew what might happen to her if she remained here?

No one argued with her.

"I take it you didn't catch him?" she asked, raising an eyebrow at Marshal Delacure.

"I didn't catch him but I called Hendrix. He's on it."

Kate submitted to being examined. Despite her recent trauma, she'd escaped relatively unscathed. Not even a cracked rib, although she had sustained some deep muscle bruising.

"You'll be achy for a few days. You can take over-the-counter pain relievers. Alternate between ibuprofen and acetaminophen every four to six hours." The doctor handed her a printed sheet of instructions. "If you have any complications or if the pain becomes unbearable, come back in."

Not likely. She'd deal with the pain.

"Marshal, I didn't get a chance to ask you before. How'd you get to us so fast at the lake?" Abram leaned against the side of the bed Kate was sitting in.

Marshal Delacure held up her cell phone, shaking it back and forth. "I was on the phone with Kate, remember? I heard some yelling and then the connection was broken. I was already on the road, heading in your direction. I might have run a red light."

Kate didn't understand Abram's snicker at first. "Katie, when we were following the ambulance, I thought we'd never get to you. She was practically going walking speed."

That startled a laugh out of both women.

Still chuckling, the marshal shook her head. "I was following the speed limit. We knew she was in good hands."

"Well," Kate inserted with a touch of sarcasm, "you thought I was in good hands. I don't suppose anyone expected that guy to attack me here. Hey, my attacker said that I'd made him look like fool in front of his boss. So he's working with someone."

The marshal's mouth tightened. "We need to get out of here. Too many things to discuss. There's no privacy here. I don't want to borrow the conference room again. I want to go somewhere different."

Kate hopped down from the bed. She grimaced. "My shoes are destroyed."

"Let me see if I can find you something."

She left them alone.

"You really scared me today."

Kate jerked her head up to stare at Abram. His face was drawn, deep grooves running the length of his tanned cheeks.

"I'm sorry."

What else could she say?

"Nothing you did on purpose. I am confused, though. Don't you have to pass a swimming test to become a cop?"

"Nah," she said, shrugging. "There's no water requirement. I have never had a reason to know how to swim before today."

She rubbed her chest. When she dropped her hand, Abram caught it and gave it a quick squeeze before releasing it. Flustered, she gave all her attention to the marshal who'd returned.

"Are you sure you're all right to leave?" the marshal asked.

"Yes, ma'am. I'll rest much better away from this place."

Marshal Delacure searched her face. Finally, she nodded slowly. "If you're sure, I'll bring the car around under the carport."

She departed, leaving them alone wrapped in silence charged with emotions. Kate wracked her brain, desperate for a lighthearted or witty comment to diffuse the tension building up. Nothing came to mind.

Deep inside, she was having trouble wrapping her mind around the concept that she'd nearly drowned. If Abram hadn't been with her, she'd be dead by now. And it wasn't an accident.

How did one cope with knowledge like that?

"I guess I'll have to learn to swim," she muttered. What a dumb thing to say.

It worked, though. She surprised a chuckle from the man standing at her side.

A nurse popped in with some thick socks. She'd have to deal with not having boots until she could locate a replacement pair. Pushing her feet into the socks, she sighed with pleasure. Cold feet were the worst.

As they moved down the hall, her shoulder blades constantly twitched. Every time someone looked her way, she wondered if any of them were out to get her.

Not knowing what had happened to Beth or what the motive was of the person or persons who had set out to murder her, everyone she met became a possible suspect.

There'd be no peace until this case was closed.

She prayed they'd find the ones responsible before either she or Abram became another statistic.

Abram placed his hand on Katie's back as he steered her through the hospital, staying close enough to interfere if anyone dared to loom too close to her. He'd never tried to be intimidating before. Amish folk were, as a rule, pacifists. He would never use a gun on another person, or another weapon. Not even to protect himself.

He would scowl at anyone who was a possible danger to her. And he would risk his own life to protect those he cared about.

He stumbled over his feet at the thought flowing through his mind.

Katie was definitely someone he cared about. More than he should. Realizing what a dangerous path his thoughts were traveling down, he removed his hand. Instantly, he missed the contact. His hand hovered above her shoulder. If someone got too close or charged at them, he'd yank her out of the way. His fingers twitched instinctively.

He hadn't deliberately failed her before, but the fact that she felt she couldn't trust him with what had happened to her filled him with shame. If she'd come to him, he wouldn't have turned her away. He certainly wouldn't have blamed her.

The fist at his side clenched. If she'd known about what had happened in his family, not only to Marta, but also to his *mamm*'s younger sister, would it have made a difference? They'd never spoken of it, the aunt who'd been abducted and murdered. It was so long ago, but the sound of his *mamm* weeping would haunt him forever.

Maybe if he'd told her about that, she would have known that his family wouldn't blame her.

They rounded the corner. Abram shook himself out of the funk he'd sunk into and tapped her shoulder.

"Almost there."

"I see it. Delacure is already waiting for us."

Indeed, through the glass doors, he made out the marshal's car. "Hope we're not in a hurry," he quipped.

She snickered. "I'd never have pegged you for the adventurous type."

He grinned. "I'm not. But if I'm going to get in a car, it should go faster than my buggy."

His buggy. Which had been probably pulled from the lake by now.

"Do you think your buggy can be salvaged?"

"I was just thinking about that. I don't think so. The front end was crumpled beyond recognition." He still didn't know how her legs hadn't been broken.

The glass doors whooshed open at their approach. The marshal was leaning against the side of her car, tapping out a text or email on her phone.

"Hey," she said, barely lifting her gaze before dropping it back to her phone. "Tim said he lost Stiles's trail. We're sure that's who we're tracking now, and your little tidbit about his boss seems to add strength to our case for him being part of the crime ring." She pocketed the phone. "We can leave if you guys are ready."

"That's not fair." Katie rolled her eyes. "We've been standing here waiting for you to finish."

"Yeah, yeah. Details, details." Straightening, the marshal sauntered around the vehicle to get in behind the steering wheel.

Abram held the front door open for Katie. She raised her brows at him. "I don't need to sit in the front."

He gestured for her to get in. Sighing, she lifted one foot and started to fold herself down into the seat.

"Hey!"

Abram tensed at the yell. Katie paused her descent. Even the marshal opened her door and exited the vehicle. Turning, Abram recognized the woman from the scuba team striding their way. She paused to look both ways before crossing the main lane into the emergency room parking lot.

Five seconds later, she joined them with a wide smile none of them returned. Katie stood up and snuggled closer to his side. Glancing down, he saw her jaw was clenched as she watched the scuba diver move closer.

Natasha. That was her name. She didn't seem to notice the wary stance of the group at the marshal's car. Her smile remained friendly, her manner easy. This was a woman trained at putting others at ease. He could easily imagine the charm and steadiness she projected helping a victim of an accident stay calm or soothing a loved one.

"Hey," she said again, halting in front of Katie. "I'm glad to see you made it. You look like you're feeling better."

Katie nodded, her face still wary. "Yeah. I'm okay. It was scary, but no lasting harm done."

"Well, that's good to hear." Natasha grabbed the

backpack slung over her shoulder. "The buggy has been pulled from the lake. I'm afraid it's not going anywhere anytime soon. That guardrail did a number on it."

He was quickly changing his mind. He would not want her to talk with anyone after a traumatic event. She had no filter.

"I got this out of the buggy." She pulled Katie's apron out. "The gun that was inside is at the police station. Evidence, I guess. I heard Lieutenant Greer saying it was a police issue."

Her curious gaze fastened onto Katie's face, bright with expectation.

Katie's features didn't change an iota. "Oh, thanks for bringing me my apron. It got stuck pretty good."

That was putting it mildly.

He might have imagined it, but Natasha's eyes tightened slightly. It was there, then it was gone. But he was correct. Something about this situation was off.

After a few more awkward moments, she left, her frustration at not getting any details obvious.

"What was with her?" Katie wondered, getting inside the marshal's car.

Marshal Delacure was dialing her phone.

"Hello?" a male voice echoed through the car's speakers. It was familiar.

"Hi, is this Lieutenant Greer?"

"You got him."

"This is Marshal Amy Delacure. I hear that Kate Bontrager's service weapon is in your evidence locker."

A loud grunt came from the speakers. "That didn't take long. Let me guess… Natasha Booth?"

"How'd you know?" Marshal Delacure eased out from beneath the carport and drove to the hospital exit.

"That woman is as nosy as they come. She thinks since she's the mayor's daughter, she has the right to know all the ins and outs of everything. She's harmless, but a nuisance."

They chatted for a few more minutes. Apparently, her gun was not in good condition due to the water, but the marshal wanted Katie to have a weapon for emergencies. Abram tuned the conversation out. He was more concerned about where they were heading.

Marshal Delacure hung up. Before she could speak, Abram said, "We can't take Katie back to the bed-and-breakfast."

Katie swerved to face him. "Where else would I stay?"

He wasn't giving in. "Katie, we have no idea who is responsible for all this. Or how it's connected to you. Or Beth. It could be nothing, but the broken bridle makes me think you are specifically a target. And they won't give up. Whether it's Gary or someone else."

"Gary?" Marshal Delacure latched onto the name. Katie blanched and squeezed her eyes shut. "Who's Gary? I think you two need to catch me up on everything that's happened. Right now."

Katie leaned her head back against the seat. He was sorry he'd mentioned the name, but still, they'd decided back at the B&B to tell the marshal about him. In a voice that cracked, Katie relayed her history with Gary, glossing over the gorier details. Marshal Delacure didn't pressure her for more. Sympathy emanated from her.

"I agree with Abram. I don't think going to the bed-and-breakfast would be wise. Not tonight when you've been attacked five times already. We know Evan Stiles is out there. It would be better to find a place to lie low. And now we have this Gary character to deal with. What did you say his last name was?"

"I didn't." Katie's chin lifted. "I never knew it. I only ever heard him referred to as Gary. In my mind, I always called him Gary the Shark."

That was as fitting a name as any.

"It's probably safe to suppose you're not the only *maidel* he attacked, ain't so?" Abram said. His stomach turned at the thought. If he'd only known, he would have supported her. He fought back a wave of red fury burning in his heart at her parents for their reaction.

"Absolutely. I'm also convinced that you're right about his ties to the human trafficking. That's something that has been more noticeable recently," Marshal Delacure said. "There have been several people who have disappeared in the past few years."

Katie sat forward. "I'm not surprised. I really hope we can put a dent in these crimes. No one should have to go through this."

"Agreed."

"We still need a place Katie can go." Abram said, smiling at her scowl.

"I'm not a civilian," Katie grated out. "I have a case to work."

"Agreed. Work it from somewhere else."

"Not the bishop's house," she stated. "Edith's expecting. I won't have that stress placed on her."

Abram's face heated. He'd been sure she was pregnant, but people didn't talk about such things.

"You can stay at my *haus*," he interrupted the discussion. He'd mentioned it to her before, and he'd meant it. There was no way he was letting her go back to the bed-and-breakfast, knowing it could very well lead her straight into a trap. The woman had been nearly killed five times in less than twenty-four hours. He wasn't eager to make it six times. He'd be able to help her and keep an eye on her better if she was close by. "*Mamm* and *Daed* won't mind."

His parents were kind people; they'd want to help Katie. Although they might have reservations if they knew how close Abram and Katie had once been. However, they'd kept their friendship private because her father tended to be strict.

David and Fanny Burkholder would be especially keen to help once they were aware that the bishop had asked Abram to help her reacclimate.

As much as he hated not giving his parents the complete truth, lives were depending on his silence regarding both Beth's and Katie's true reasons for returning to the community. In a very short time, she may well be on her way back to Wallmer Grove.

He'd do his best to help her, and then he'd let her go.

It might just break his heart for good.

NINE

Abram gave Marshal Delacure his address. She tapped it into her GPS. He would have preferred to give directions verbally, but she'd waved the offer aside and said it would be easier to use her phone.

"Abram."

He turned his head to look at Katie and raised his eyebrows, waiting for her to continue. She bit her lip, looking unsure. When she shook her head, he knew she'd decided to wait until they were alone.

Alone with Katie. He'd been alone with her several times. His heart sped up. She was getting to him again, but it was different now. When they'd been friends before, he'd thought he'd known everything about her. They were so happy and so naive. Neither was prepared for the curve in the road that tore them apart.

He was getting to know the woman she'd become. If he weren't careful, he'd fall in love with her all over again. He flinched. Katie Bontrager was more than a beautiful woman. She was that. But she was also fierce, intelligent and brave.

She claimed her faith had been destroyed. He disagreed. When she'd asked him to pray, he'd seen the light and hope flickering in her face.

She still had faith. It was buried but it was there. If only he could help her bring it back completely. Faith was something too personal for that. It had to be between her and *Gott*, although he would definitely do his best to flame the spark to life.

That didn't mean she was back in his life.

It was late afternoon when they arrived back at his *haus*. His *mamm* would have dinner almost ready to set on the table. His brother Sam would be home by now with their *daed*. They usually arrived home around four on Thursday afternoons. His twenty-three-year-old brother was still single. He had shown some interest in a young lady a few years back, but nothing came of it.

His *daed* came out on the porch when they pulled into the driveway. His bushy salt-and-pepper eyebrows shot into his hairline when he spied Abram riding in a car.

"I'm not looking forward to telling *Daed* where the buggy is." He put his hand on the door handle to exit the car.

"He'll be happy to know you're well," Katie stated.

"*Ja*. That he will."

The marshal's phone rang as she shifted into Park. She took the phone off the speaker setting and answered it, her voice tense. "I have to go. You two all right?"

"*Ja*." If he weren't safe at his home, where would he be safe?

She waited until they were both standing outside in the damp weather before shifting into Reverse and easing down the driveway.

"Riding in a car with her is almost as frustrating as anything else that's happened to us today," Katie quipped, shaking her head. "If I knew her better, I'd have offered to drive. Seriously, did you see how slow she was driving?"

He nodded as they turned and moved toward his father. "I could have walked home faster."

She snickered. Her laughter fled as they approached and were caught by his father's stare. David Burkholder was intimidating and had a stern manner, but after seeing him interact with his grandchildren, Abram had lost the awe he'd felt when he was younger.

"Where's the buggy, Abram?" David asked. "I know you took it this morning."

"*Ja*. Well, we had an accident," Abram hedged. His *daed* would need to know eventually what had happened, but right now he needed to keep it simple. "The bridle broke and the buggy ended up in Lake Sutter. We're fine, but the buggy is in bad shape."

At the word *we*, his father's gaze flashed to Katie. It had been ten years since he'd seen her, so maybe he wouldn't recognize her.

"Katie? Katie Bontrager?"

His *mamm* was coming through the door. Her progress was slow due to her arthritis, but she wouldn't complain or ask for help unless it was absolutely necessary. She gasped as her husband spoke their guest's name.

"*Ach!* Katie! We all worried so when you left, ain't so, Abram?"

He flushed. His parents obviously hadn't been as unaware of his relationship as he'd thought. "*Ja*, is so."

He needed to change the course of this conversation,

fast. "*Mamm, Daed*, Katie needs somewhere to stay. Bishop Hershberger asked me to help her."

Before they could respond, Katie took charge of the conversation, derailing his plans to keep it simple.

"Actually, I think you should know that someone is trying to kill me." Her chin tilted and firmed. "Someone cut the bridle on your horse, which is how the buggy ended up in the lake."

"I wasn't going to tell them that," Abram complained. "The bishop—"

"Didn't tell *me* not to say anything."

Her defiant expression told him what she couldn't say. She wouldn't let him omit the truth and deceive his family. Warmth burst in his chest. As much as he was trying to protect her, she was doing the same for him. He dipped his head once in a silent gesture of appreciation, hoping she'd understand.

The older couple gaped at them, eyes wide with shock, for a full thirty seconds before either of them attempted to speak. David started and stopped twice before turning his head to his wife.

Fanny moved closer to Katie and pulled her in a gentle hug, Katie was a full three inches taller than his *mamm*, but that didn't matter as she bowed her head and allowed the older woman to comfort her.

But only for a few seconds. She straightened and backed away, moving until she was again at his side. His fingers twitched, the urge to reach out and claim her hand battling with his good sense. It hurt not to have the right to offer the same comfort and care that she accepted from his mother.

"*Cumme.* Let's go into the *haus* where it's warm." David helped his wife back up the stairs. "Don't worry

Loyal Readers
FREE BOOKS Voucher

We're giving away **THOUSANDS** of **FREE BOOKS**

Romance

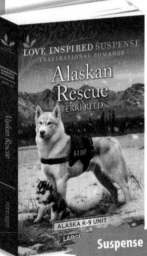

Suspense

Don't Miss Out! Send for Your Free Books Today!

Get up to 4
FREE FABULOUS BOOKS
You Love!

To thank you for being a loyal reader we'd like to send you up to 4 FREE BOOKS, absolutely free.

Just write "YES" on the Loyal Reader Voucher and we'll send you up to 4 Free Books and Free Mystery Gifts, altogether worth over $20, as a way of saying thank you for being a loyal reader.

Try **Love Inspired® Romance Larger-Print** books and fall in love with inspirational romances that take you on an uplifting journey of faith, forgiveness and hope.

Try **Love Inspired® Suspense Larger-Print** books where courage and optimism unite in stories of faith and love in the face of danger.

Or **TRY BOTH!**

We are so glad you love the books as much as we do and can't wait to send you great new books.

So don't miss out, return your Loyal Reader Voucher Today!

Pam Powers

LOYAL READER
FREE BOOKS VOUCHER

YES! I Love Reading, please send me up to 4 FREE BOOKS and Free Mystery Gifts from the series I select.

Just write in "YES" on the dotted line below then return this card today and we'll send your free books & gifts asap!

➡️ YES ⬅️

Which do you prefer?

☐ Love Inspired® Romance Larger-Print 122/322 IDL GRJD	☐ Love Inspired® Suspense Larger-Print 107/307 IDL GRJD	☐ BOTH 122/322 & 107/307 IDL GRJP

FIRST NAME

LAST NAME

ADDRESS

APT.#

CITY

STATE/PROV.

ZIP/POSTAL CODE

EMAIL ☐ Please check this box if you would like to receive newsletters and promotional emails from Harlequin Enterprises ULC and its affiliates. You can unsubscribe anytime.

LI/SLI-520-LR21

HARLEQUIN Reader Service —**Here's how it works:**

about the buggy, Abram. We have another, and even if we didn't, *Gott* always provides."

Abram nodded his agreement to his father, then quietly watched as the older couple mounted the stairs. His mouth tightened. His *mamm*'s arthritis was steadily worsening. She would be pleased when either he or Sam married and took over the *haus* so she and his *daed* could move into the *dawdi haus*. His oldest brother Levi had gotten married several years ago. He had never joined the family painting business, though, so he had built his bride a *haus* and they now lived a short distance from the rest of the family. Which turned out to be for the best, as his brother had recently been elected a deacon in the church. He needed to have his own place. *Nee*, it would be up to either himself or Sam to relieve their parents' burdens.

Instinctively, his eyes flew to the woman beside him.

It was too easy to see her as his wife.

He needed to get a grip and fast. No matter how much she made him yearn, it could never be.

Abram was troubled. He didn't appear angry, but the distress furrowed his forehead. Maybe she shouldn't have announced to his parents that she was a walking target. While she appreciated his attempt to guard her secret, it wouldn't be fair to stay in the Burkholder house without informing her hosts that she came with some serious baggage.

If anything happened to Abram or his family, it would devastate her. She half hoped they would tell her, *Sorry, you can't stay here, after all*. It wouldn't happen.

Instead of sitting down to discuss the events of the

day, Fanny asked Katie if she wouldn't mind helping to set the table for dinner. Astonished, Katie nodded, confused. Were they going to ignore what she'd said? Fanny intercepted the look she exchanged with Abram. Passing Katie a stack of bowls, the older woman nodded toward the table.

As the woman moved to the stove, Katie could see her swollen knuckles and the painful way she moved. Katie wanted to offer to help, but didn't want to offend her. She'd seen how both Abram and David had watched her with love and concern. They'd been discreet in the ways they'd assisted her.

"Don't worry. We'll talk about your troubles, Katie." Kate was bemused. Fanny said *troubles* as if what had been going on was a simple matter, rather than the stuff of horror novels.

Fanny took a large wooden spoon and stirred the fragrant soup in a pot on the stove. "Whatever you tell us won't change our decision. You are here, and you need a safe place to rest. I know you and Abram were friends long ago. Since the bishop has asked him to help you, and he brought you here, the matter is settled, *ja*?"

It was so typical of David and Fanny to be so generous and practical. Growing up, they'd always been that way, willing to share what they had with anyone in need. She should have expected it. She turned to hide her stinging eyes, blinking frantically. Her own *mamm* and *daed* had not been so understanding, ever. If they had been...

Shaking her head furiously, she set a bowl on the table harder than necessary.

"Sorry," she muttered.

Turning her head, she saw Fanny had left the room for a moment. Abram stepped next to her and slid an arm across her shoulders, giving her a slight squeeze before releasing her. Warmth tingled down her back. It soothed her, even when he moved away.

Rubbing the moisture from her lashes, she smiled at Fanny when she returned.

When dinner was announced, Katie sat with the rest of the family. David bowed his head, indicating it was time for each person at the table to say a silent prayer of thanksgiving. Katie bowed her head, but her mind was blank. The desire to pray sprang up unexpectedly. She struggled to formulate the appropriate words. In the end, she settled for, *Thanks. Please help.* It wasn't poetry, but it was a cry straight from her tormented soul.

Talk at the dinner table was minimal. Abram's brother Sam ate like he was starving and hadn't eaten in days. David teased his son about it.

"You should have packed a bigger lunch, my *sohn*. I don't want you withering away."

"Daed." The younger man flushed, flicking an embarrassed glance toward Kate.

Abram joined in the fun. "A bigger lunch? *Daed*, he had two sandwiches, a banana, two of *mamm*'s cookies and a bag of chopped carrots and celery."

"Ja, I know this. He also finished the cookies your *mamm* had packed for me."

She might have felt bad for Sam except he was soon laughing with the rest of the family. *"Ja*, but I was hungry! We did a lot of *gut* hard work today, *Daed.*"

"That we did."

She'd never had a conversation such as this with her parents. After her sisters had married, she'd been the only one home with her *mamm* and *daed*. Kate had never understood why they'd been so strict and disapproving with her. It seemed that she had spent her entire life trying to please them and getting slapped down again. Maybe that's why her sisters were both so quick to leave and didn't visit. They'd both been so much older than Kate that there hadn't been much of a relationship.

The only one she'd been close to in her family was long gone. Her brother, John, had been ten months older than Kate. They'd grown up as if they were twins, and then suddenly when he was ten, John grew ill and he'd died of leukemia when she was twelve.

Just one more loss in her life.

When the meal concluded, Sam went out to the barn to feed the animals and finish a project he'd been working on. Kate helped Fanny clean up, then she joined Abram and his parents at the table to discuss what had been happening.

When they heard further about the buggy, they were appalled to hear how close she'd come to dying. When she told them that Abram had performed CPR, they turned wide eyes to their son.

"You saved her."

Abram squirmed. She smiled at how shy he was about accepting praise. "Levi taught me last month. I never understood why he had insisted that I learn it."

"Ja." David nodded his head sagely. *"Gott* inspired your brother. He knew that you would need to use that. It's amazing how He works things out for our *gut."*

"Not always." She hadn't meant to blurt that out. Her mind had spun onto her experience as a teen and she'd been unable to react to it. "Sorry. I don't mean to be rude."

Fanny heaved her slight frame out of her chair and walked with a crooked, hobbling gait to where Kate sat, ignoring David's and Abram's exclamations. Waving their concern away, she settled into the chair next to Kate, sitting close enough to loop an arm behind the younger woman's back. Kate's instincts told her to lean in closer to the comfort offered, but she resisted.

"Katie. *Gott* never abandoned you. He never took His eyes off you. You may never know why those horrible things happened. What we do know is that *Gott* kept you in the palm of His hand and brought you out of it."

Abram murmured, "You're one of the strongest people I know, Katie."

She struggled with this new way of thinking.

David leaned in. "Remember the prophet Jeremiah? He endured much. In chapter twenty-nine, we read, *For I know the thoughts that I think toward you, saith the Lord, thoughts of peace, and not of evil, to give you an expected end.*"

Slowly nodding, she voiced the thoughts brewing in your mind. "So, you're saying that God allows things to happen, but He still works it out so it's best for us?"

"Well," Abram said, scratching his head, "I know that we have to suffer in life. And think about it. If we didn't suffer, would we even understand how much we needed *Gott*?"

They were no longer talking only about the incident at the lake. Abram was telling her God still loved her, and had cared for her, even during the darkest moments of her life. Did she believe that? Could she allow herself to trust Him again?

"I'm scared," she admitted to Abram. "You say I'm strong, but I don't think I'm capable of handling too much more."

"You've heard that verse from Philippians that says, *I can do all things through Christ which strengtheneth me*?"

She laughed. It emerged like a short bark. "Ugh. I haven't opened a Bible in ten years. I'll have to find that one."

She'd shocked her hosts. Still, they were gracious about it. David brought the Bible and opened it to the fourth chapter of Philippians and placed his finger beside verse thirteen. She read that verse, then she read the next one. And the next. It was beautiful and spoke to her like no book ever had. Turning to the beginning of the chapter, she read the title and author's name.

"I don't recall ever reading any of this," she exclaimed. "I've heard of the Apostle Paul, of course. But this is all new to me."

Abram blessed her with a beatific smile. Her breath caught. "The Bible is a wondrous thing, *ja*?"

Her mind was going to explode if she sat for very much longer. She needed to move around.

Abram stood. "*Cumme*. You look like you could use a break."

How did he do that? He knew exactly what she needed. Was she that transparent, or was their connection still there? She wasn't sure how she felt about that. Her feelings were getting all scrambled up inside her. Before she would have tried to reject the connection. Now, it was something that helped her keep going.

Excusing themselves, Abram and Kate stood. Impulsively, Kate leaned down and hugged Fanny, hard. Abram's mother squeezed back. Whew. The older woman had more strength left in her pain-ridden body than her family knew.

Abram held the door open for her and they walked out into the dusk. Soon, the day would be gone. Kate wouldn't be sorry to put this day behind her. It had been terrifying and unsettling in too many ways.

Breathing deep, she smiled at the scents in the air. She loved the smell of the earth after a rainfall. The sky was still cloudy. She knew more rain was to come. It was hurricane season, after all. While they wouldn't get much in the way of destructive wind or rains, they'd have a few days of harsher than normal weather.

It had also brought her a small measure of peace, though. Awareness of Abram strolling quietly at her side sang through her. She'd never let another man get this close to her before. The idea of doing so made her grimace. No, Abram Burkholder was a special man. She'd liked him as a young girl. But as a woman, she appreciated the sense of security and restfulness he exuded. He was not a man who postured or bragged to bring attention to himself.

He was Abram, plain and simple. That was enough.

Unfortunately, it wouldn't be enough to save his life. She'd have to double her efforts to keep her distance. She couldn't allow a mistake on her part to cost him everything.

TEN

Abram kept his hands clasped behind his back to resist the urge to reach for her hand. Katie was still with him, and that was wondrously *gut*, but she wasn't his. Not like he wanted her to be. The way things were now, she never would be.

He'd seen her sidewise glances at him, despite her attempt to be discreet. Katie was resisting the same temptations. He was sure of it.

But they were both hindered by the lives they'd chosen. Having her with him, for a few days or a few hours, it had to be sufficient. For while he could easily fall in love with the lovely and courageous woman his Katie had grown into, he could never leave his world for her.

Not because she wasn't worthy of his devotion. She absolutely was. But he had made a promise to *Gott*. His faith was more to him than being with his family and living a simple life. *Nee*, his faith was about service to his *Gott* with his whole heart. That had to come before work, before family. Before love.

They were at a stalemate.

"Why didn't you ever marry?" The question floated softly on the fall air. So soft, he might have imagined it.

It wasn't a question he was enthusiastic to answer. Especially in light of their growing attraction. She had told him about Gary, though. Could he really deny her this?

He cleared his throat. The one positive about the dimming light was it would hide his crimson ears. "Well, I just never did. I walked out once. With Edith's cousin, Linda."

She gasped softly. "I remember Linda. She was always kind. Kind of shy, but nice. I didn't know her well."

He smiled. He'd heard the trace of jealousy that she hadn't been able to disguise. His smile faltered. It wasn't good to encourage jealousy, or any other emotions dealing with affection.

"*Ja*, she was sweet and kind. She was also unwilling to settle. I asked her to marry me. My family had already decided we'd make a *gut* couple." He shrugged, then he amended his answer. "Not all of my family. Levi, he didn't think we'd suit. He told me not to be too hasty. I didn't listen, of course. Levi's a great guy, but this was my decision."

She stopped and turned toward him. "What happened? It obviously didn't work out."

He gazed up out at the horizon before pivoting to meet her gaze. "She turned me down because I didn't love her. She thought I had someone else. I didn't. I'd just never moved on from you and hadn't realized it until that moment."

She gasped and backed away, shaking her head. Her blue eyes glistened in the twilight. "Abram!"

Even her voice was broken.

"Shhh." He closed the distance between them. "It's not your fault. You can't take the blame for what happened in my life."

"But I am to blame! Abram, I shut you out. I was so scared of your reaction, so ashamed, that I turned away from you, from God. I never even tried to connect with my sisters. I just ran. Like a coward."

He wasn't having that. Fisting his hands so they wouldn't reach out to hold her close, he kept his voice low, trying to soothe her with his gentleness.

"You are not, and have never been, a coward. I wish I'd known how things were with you, but you were always the one who was the first to volunteer for a new venture, or the one who dreamed of becoming a missionary. I never really wanted more than to stay here and work in my *daed*'s painting business."

"That was a good dream. I guess we never know how life will end up." She paused. "When I told you Beth had been attacked, you were shocked. I thought that meant that you might not react well."

Startled, he jerked back. "*Nee!* That wasn't it at all!"

Shooting a quick glance at his *haus* to be sure his parents weren't listening, he told her about his cousin. "She's *gut* now and has two sweet *kinder* with her husband."

"It's possible to move on, then." The wistful edge in her voice was nearly his undoing.

"Remember. With *Gott*, all things are possible."

Rather than replying, she changed the subject to more mundane topics. He let it go, not wanting to force his faith on her. He'd planted a seed and seen some interest sprout. He'd step back and let *Gott* do the rest.

They made plans to go back to Beth's *haus* the next

day so she could look around. Then she wanted to go to the bed-and-breakfast to see if she could find out anything from those working with Beth.

"Besides, I have a room there. It would look odd if I never used it."

He didn't know about that. He'd try to persuade her to check out when they went.

Before he went to bed, he said a quick prayer for her healing and for *Gott* to teach her to give herself grace. The peace that flowed through him as he closed his eyes soothed his soul. *Ja, Gott* would take care of his Katie.

The next morning, Katie greeted him with a groan. Concerned, he pulled out a chair for her at the breakfast table. She didn't look well.

"Katie? What's wrong? You're very pale this morning."

She grimaced. "Sorry. I'm just feeling very bruised today. It's still a little painful to breathe, although not as bad as it was yesterday in the hospital."

"Why don't you rest this morning? I'll be home this afternoon, and we can go then."

"I don't like waiting, but I think you might have a good plan," she admitted.

Satisfied, Abram kissed his *mamm* on the cheek; he headed out the back door and to the barn before he gave in to the temptation to kiss Katie's cheek, too. *Daed* and Sam had already left for their jobsite, catching a ride with a neighbor. Despite Abram's protests, his father had insisted he take the buggy since he needed to help Katie after work.

"Just don't let this one end up in Lake Sutter," Sam had joked.

Abram rolled his eyes in response.

He hitched up his mare to the buggy, keeping an eye on the weather. He didn't like the look of the sky. During the night, the rain had started again. At first, it was a light sprinkle, but as the night had continued on, the wind kicked up. The earth had a little extra give to it when he stepped on the grass. By the time the mare was hitched up, his boots were muddy from the soggy ground. As he drove toward town, he saw the evidence of the storm. Every now and then, he'd see a *haus* with a shingle or two missing. Branches littered the road, kicked aside by the mare's hooves. He tried to steer her around the worst, but there were so many of them.

The rain had slowed, but the sky was heavy with the promise of more. Dark clouds moved rapidly across the sky, spinning and swirling like an angry swarm of honeybees guarding the queen.

At the jobsite, he joined the other employee on the project. Briefly, they discussed what needed to be done and prepped the area. It was good that they were working on an indoor project. If it had been outside, they would have needed to cancel it due to the weather. Hurricane season often brought more rain and high winds. Maybe even a flash flood or two.

The weather report warned that they might get an unprecedented amount of precipitation this week. He frowned at that.

Katie was fine at his *haus*. He wished she would stay there, but she wasn't planning on it. At least he'd convinced her to let him go with her. He glanced at the sky again. Although, they might be wiser to wait a few days.

That probably wasn't an option. Not with Beth out there somewhere.

He pulled his thoughts away from her. Katie knew how to take care of herself. *Mamm* was with her, so she wasn't alone. And now that Marshal Delacure was aware of their concerns, Katie would be watched over. He could stop worrying and focus on his job.

The sky looked worse when he left. He frowned. His *daed* had asked him to get lumber. If he waited too long, it might not come in time. Abram decided to stop by the lumberyard on his way home to place an important order.

"Hey ya, Abram." Isaiah, the owner, was standing by the door, wiping his hands on a less-than-clean rag while he surveyed the sky. "I'm thinking this storm might be a doozy."

Abram nodded. "*Ja. Daed* was talking to some *Englischers* we're doing an indoor job for. They were talking about visiting their *kinder* in Indiana until the system passed. Overkill, do you suppose? We don't usually get much here."

Isaiah frowned. "I don't know. We're going to be getting more rain than usual. I know the farmers are concerned."

Abram glared up at the dark sky. "Have you been selling more lumber than usual?"

"*Ja*, business has been *gut*. What can I get for you?"

Abram made his order and paid Isaiah. By the time he left, he was more than an hour late for meeting Katie. He shrugged. It couldn't be helped. As soon as he got home, they'd head out.

Kate watched the darkening sky out the window with concern. Where was Abram? He was supposed to be home an hour ago. She sighed. The windows shiv-

ered as a blast of wind hit them. The water was beginning to come down in waves.

Turning back to the house, she tried to think what
she could do.

Abram wouldn't like it if she left without him. Not
that she could do that, anyway. He was her only way
to get anywhere. If only she had a car…

But she didn't. Nor did she have a phone anymore to
call for a driver. She thought about that. Some Amish
families had phones in their garages for business pur-
poses. She had no idea if David had such a phone. If he
did, and she called a driver, would that settle Abram's
concerns regarding her being alone?

She looked across the room at Abram's mother.
Fanny was sitting down, calmly sewing a garment as
if the wind and the rain didn't disturb her at all. It probably didn't; her faith was such an integral part of her
life. What would it be like to have such confidence
that God would make everything work out? That even
when bad things happened, good could come from it?

She used to have faith. She swallowed, trying to dis-
lodge the lump in her throat. It did no good to repine.
She couldn't undo the past.

Kate returned to the window in time to see a vehicle pull in. Recognizing Marshal Delacure's car, her
spirits lightened. Maybe she could ask the marshal to
accompany her. Then Abram couldn't complain that
she was alone. Nor would she have to sit beside him,
longing for more than she could ever have.

If only…

That was useless. She couldn't change the past. She
could only move forward. Although, she hadn't done

that very well so far. Instinctively, she reached out to God mentally, asking for His guidance.

Had He listened? She never doubted that He could hear her. She just hadn't been sure He'd bother with her small concerns. A sense of peace, just a tiny nugget, unfurled inside her.

A knock at the door interrupted her musings. "I'll get it, Fanny. It's the marshal I'm working with."

Quickly moving through the kitchen, she got to the door and opened it.

"Hey, Kate. I'm glad I caught you in."

Kate stepped back and invited the marshal in. Fanny walked slowly into the room to welcome the visitor. When the marshal glanced at Kate, she nodded. "It's okay. Abram's parents know I'm a cop and that I'm here to help you with something, with the bishop's permission."

Spitting out the awkward sentence, she waited. The marshal nodded with approval, her eyes crinkling as she smiled at Fanny. Kate had managed to give her most of the major details she and Abram had shared. The marshal was now aware that they knew she was a cop, but unaware of Beth and her real purpose in coming.

"I did need to talk with you for a few minutes, Kate."

"Sure." She bit her lip. How did she ask Marshal Delacure to give her a ride to Beth's and the B&B?

Widening her eyes, she looked out at the car. The marshal got the hint.

"Would you be able to come with me for a drive?"

"Of course!"

The marshal grinned, her eyebrows shooting up.

Maybe her response was a little too enthusiastic. She flushed.

"I'll let Abram know you're with a friend," Fanny offered.

"Thanks, Fanny. Hopefully, I'll be back by dinnertime."

Marshal Delacure glanced at her watch. "It's only two. I'm sure we can manage that. I have a five o'clock appointment."

Kate nodded. Three hours should be enough time. The police had already gone through Beth's house. She didn't know what else she expected to find there, but there was an off chance that maybe something had been missed.

Or maybe Beth had returned at some point. She knew that wasn't likely, but every avenue had to be checked out. Gathering the cloak the bishop had given her, Kate said her goodbye to Fanny and trailed after Marshal Delacure.

Once they were both buckled into the vehicle, the marshal did a shaky three-point turn and departed from the Burkholder *haus*.

"I'm glad you were able to get away. I've been stewing over this case all morning and decided I wanted to have another go at looking around Beth's house. I thought you might be helpful. It's never a good idea to check in on a crime scene alone."

Kate laughed, relieved. "I was wanting to go look around, but I didn't have a phone to call you. Abram had planned to help me look around, but he must have been detained at work."

"It's probably best not to bring him any further into

it. We'll be better off with the two of us." Marshal Delacure adjusted the radio, turning it down so it was background noise.

That was probably true, but Kate felt odd leaving without him. She didn't object, though. "If we don't find anything useful at Beth's house, then I think we should go over to the bed-and-breakfast and talk with her coworkers. However, I'm inclined to leave that until I have Abram with me, since the place is owned by his relatives."

"I can go along with that plan." The marshal stepped on the gas and drove toward the house that her missing witness had been living in.

Kate held back a snarky comment congratulating the marshal on almost driving the speed limit. It was the kind of remark she could make with her partner. Or with Abram. She wasn't sure about the marshal and she didn't want to offend her. Plus, the marshal didn't have to invite her to help out. It would have been easy enough for her to tag the Sutter Springs police department. Lieutenant Greer already had some idea of what was going on. She had to appreciate that.

When they arrived at the house, both women sat in the car for a moment, peering around them, trying to see if there was any danger. Not seeing anything out of place, they looked at each other and nodded. At the same time, they put their hands on the door handles and stepped from the car.

"Are we sure there are no more bombs?" Kate asked, somewhat nervous after her previous experience.

"Well, as of yesterday there was nothing. Lieutenant

Greer made sure to give the place a thorough sweep. I think we can go inside without any risk."

Kate quirked her right eyebrow at the other woman. "Do you think he'd get his nose out of joint if he knew we were here?"

She had a healthy respect for law enforcement, being a cop herself, and she really didn't want to step on the local police officer's toes again.

Marshal Delacure laughed. "Relax! I called him myself this morning and told him that I might be bringing you over here."

Kate grinned. The other woman had figured her out fairly quickly.

"Oh, before I forget." The marshal reached into her pocket. "The second reason I came out was to give you this. Here's a new phone you can use. I already plugged some important numbers in it. The marshals paid for it since you lost your previous phone helping us."

"Thanks." Kate accepted the phone gratefully and slipped it into the pocket in her apron. Investigating Beth's disappearance, and Gary, would be smoother with easy access to a phone with internet capabilities.

Together, the women made their way slowly up the front steps of the house. It felt strange entering an Amish house by the front door, but the back porch had been completely demolished so there wasn't really any choice. Inside the house, they allowed their eyes to acclimate to the change in lighting.

"Wow!" Katie turned in a full circle. "When you guys said someone had ransacked her house, you weren't kidding. I don't think there's a place we can step where we won't tromp all over Beth's belongings."

"Yeah, I know. Kind of sad." The marshal frowned and scanned the room they were in. "We don't have that much time. Tell you what, you take the upstairs and I'll take the downstairs."

Kate really didn't want to be separated. Suddenly, she wished Abram had come with her. Nonsense. She would be fine. This was a routine procedure. Putting on a show of confidence she so did not feel, Kate nodded and strode over to the stairs. As she moved up the stairs, her stomach sank lower with each step upward she took.

It wasn't a large house. She finished with the first room and started on the second. There were papers everywhere. It was a bit overwhelming. Not to mention how rude it felt to be going through someone else's things. But she had a job to do. Kate shoved aside her misgivings and pulled a dresser drawer out. As she had suspected, the drawer itself was empty, all of its contents having already been spilled on the floor.

She tried to push it back in. It wouldn't move. Frowning, she tried to shut it again with more force.

It was completely jammed. Pulling the drawer out and completely removing it from the tracks, she carefully brought the drawer over to the bed and turned it upside down.

A letter-sized envelope was taped to the bottom of the drawer.

Excitement coursed through her. This could be the break they were searching for. Holding her breath, she carefully removed the envelope. It had been taped shut. Working slowly, she opened it, taking care not to damage the contents.

She hissed as she read the contents.

Beth had been playing sleuth. She'd talked with the family and friends of Ishmael, the boy who'd overdosed. She'd also talked with the families of other victims, parents who had insisted their child was being forced to sell drugs.

She turned the paper over. Her eyes widened. Beth had also been keeping track of Gary's comings and goings. His name was Gary Lloyd, and Kate wasn't the only one to suspect him of being more than a deliveryman. She'd apparently saved another young girl from him after hearing what was possibly a kidnapping plot. The girl had had no idea she was a target when Beth asked her to switch schedules.

Later that night, she'd gone to see Lieutenant Greer.

Katie froze.

He had acted like he knew nothing about what was going on. Obviously, the man had lied.

A lot of new questions burst into her mind. What game was the lieutenant playing? Had he lied about not knowing who Beth was?

A shiver passed through Kate. She recalled hearing that witnesses were only ever in danger if they broke the rules. Had she broken the rules? Had Beth revealed her secrets to the lieutenant in a quest to protect the local kids?

Suddenly, she realized that she couldn't hear anything downstairs. Stepping gently so as not to make any noise, Kate moved to the door and pressed her ear against it. Nothing. A chill swept through her that had nothing to do with the cold. At the very least, she should hear Marshal Delacure moving around. Had something happened to the other woman?

A creak coming from the base of the stairs caught her attention. Followed by a muffled exclamation. She stiffened. Marshal Delacure's voice was higher and distinctly female.

There was a man in the house, and it wasn't Abram.

ELEVEN

Abram drove home through the heavy rain and violent wind. Every gust pushed against his buggy. The mare put her head down against the resistance. Her ears were pinned back. Steering in these conditions was dicey. When he arrived home, he'd need to tell Katie that they might have to hold off on their trip to Beth's *haus*. He hated to disappoint her, but it was best to stay home in this weather.

She'd be upset with the change of plans, but he was hoping she'd understand. After all, he couldn't justify risking their lives or putting his mare in danger when they could go the next morning. He'd ask *daed* if he could skip work and take her around. That way, they'd have the full day to search. He'd go wherever she wanted to go without a single complaint.

Surely, that would be sufficient.

He unhitched the horse and swiftly rubbed her down. After she was taken care of, he put the tack away in its proper place. Holding his hat on his head, he made a mad dash from the barn to the *haus* to avoid getting wet, but also to see Katie. He couldn't explain his sudden anxiety, but he wanted her to know that she could rely on him. Showing up over an hour late probably wasn't the best way to go about that. On the porch, he shook off as much water as he could before stomping off his boots and opening the door.

Entering the *haus*, he set his hat on the peg and moved into the main part of the *haus*. His *mamm* was in the front room. He greeted her distractedly as he noticed Katie wasn't in the room. Frowning, he walked through the *haus* as he searched for Katie. She was probably upstairs in the room she'd slept in the night before.

Still uneasy, he shrugged. He could wait a few more minutes to talk with her. He couldn't explain the edginess that had him pacing in front of the large picture window. He was bone tired, but the moment he lowered himself into a chair, his agitated nerves had him shooting back up to begin pacing again.

He spent a few more minutes conversing with his mother, telling her about his day. All the while, he was listening for Katie.

Finally, he couldn't stand it any longer. "Is Katie upstairs?"

"Oh," she said as her hand flew to his mouth. "I forgot. Her marshal friend came over and asked her to go for a drive. That was about forty minutes ago."

A cold sweat broke out on his forehead. He knew the marshal was a capable woman, but he had a bad feeling about this.

"*Mamm*, I gotta go. When *Daed* gets home, if I'm not back, have him go to the emergency box and call the police. Send them to Beth Zook's *haus*."

Grabbing his hat, he darted out the door and flew off the porch, completely bypassing the steps. Running to the barn, he re-hitched his mare. Even if he was wrong and everything was fine, he'd rather take the chance rather than not and find out later that she'd needed him.

"Sorry, girl. I'd wait but Katie might be in trouble." He'd never tacked up a horse as quick in his life. Hopping into the buggy, he twitched the reins to start the mare moving. Obediently, the animal started forward.

Beth's *haus* was only a few minutes away. Anxiety raced through his system like a fire through dry leaves. He reminded himself that they'd be there soon.

He knew it would be slow going. Uttering a quick prayer, he pleaded *Gott* to let him arrive in time. If only the wind would cooperate. When the wind died down, he sent a prayer of gratitude and praise up. Only *Gott* would be able to answer his prayer and calm the weather, allowing him to push the horse to a quicker trot.

When he pulled in the drive at Beth's *haus*, Marshal Delacure's car was there. There was no sight of either the marshal or Katie outside the house. Jumping down out of the buggy, he looked around. There were footprints leading to the barn. The ground was so muddy it was difficult to decipher if the prints were going to or away from the barn. He couldn't even tell if it was one set of prints going back and forth, or multiple people walking.

Caution told him to keep down out of sight. It took all his patience, but he followed the path, trying to stay to the side of the *haus* and closer to the woodpile. He didn't want anyone to look out of the barn and see him coming. He skimmed along the edge of the property, ignoring the branches that grabbed at his hat and his shirt. A sharp thorn dragged at his sleeve, ripping the fabric and tearing at the skin underneath. He didn't slow down. Sap was tangled in his hair, but he didn't care. The only thing on his mind was getting to Katie. Every step he took brought a deeper conviction that she was in trouble and needed him.

After a few minutes of creeping closer, he reached the barn. He could hear something moving around inside it but wasn't sure what, or who, it was.

Rising up slowly, he peered inside the window. All he could see was a pair of feet wearing a rather feminine pair of boots, tied at her ankles.

Not Katie. Dashing around the corner, he swooped into the barn and crossed to the marshal, who was glaring up at him, her mouth covered with duct tape. He took out his pocketknife and sliced through the rope at her wrists. She tore the tape from her face with a grimace.

"Where's Katie?" he demanded.

"I don't know." She was already working on her feet. "Someone came up behind me while I was searching the lower level of the house. I think I must have lost consciousness for a few minutes. When I came to, I was out here like this. Kate is working on searching the upstairs." She looked up at him, and for the first time he saw fear in her gaze. More than anything else, that unnerved him. "I haven't heard anything from the house."

His pulse ramped up and blood pounded in his ears. Whoever had ambushed Marshal Delacure was possibly in the *haus* with Katie right now. He had to get in there.

"I need to go to her. Are you okay if I leave?" He poised to run the moment she gave him a sign that she was fine.

"Wait. I'm the marshal." She stood and immediately

leaned against the wall, her face pale. "Go! Kate might be in danger. I'll get there as soon as I can."

He took off without another word.

He ran as fast as his legs would carry him. The juicy mud hampered his progress. Twice, he slipped on his way to the *haus*. The first time, he teetered and then caught his balance. The second time, he was unable to compensate and he went down, the wet puddles splashing him from his feet to the top of his head. Sputtering, he rose, wiping the mud from his eyes. He couldn't stop. He picked himself up and he was off again, racing to the *haus*.

A police car pulled into the yard. Lieutenant Greer was behind the wheel. The car had barely squealed to a stop when the lieutenant threw open the door and launched himself toward the *haus*. Abram was so happy to see him. His *daed* had gotten his message!

His instinct told him to go straight into the *haus*. Lieutenant Greer, however, gestured for him to wait. Impatiently, Abram tapped his boot on the ground while he waited for the lawman to join him. Greer had his weapon out.

"Where are the women?" he rasped out, his voice raw.

Abram pointed his thumb back over his shoulder. "The marshal was ambushed as she searched the downstairs. She's in the barn. A bit unsteady, but she's alert. Katie is in the *haus*. Possibly with the man who tied up the marshal."

Lieutenant Greer edged in front of Abram. "Stay out here."

Abram ignored him and fell in line behind him. Lieutenant Greer gave him an aggravated glare but didn't protest. Time was critical now.

* * *

Katie heard footsteps clomping up the stairs. They were heavy, further proof that it wasn't Marshal Delacure. She pulled herself deeper inside the room. There was nowhere for her to hide. Recalling the letter in her hands, she folded it and slid it into the pocket of her apron where she'd normally carry her service weapon.

What she wouldn't give to have her gun on her now! While she didn't revel in the idea of using a weapon against anyone, she knew that if she had one, the chances of needing to use it would be slim. Most criminals she'd dealt with had surrendered when looking at the gun in her capable hands.

However, since she didn't have it, she'd have to rely on her other skills and her wits.

Her nerves were stretched taut as the person running stopped at the first door. Was it Evan Stiles? Had he come back to finish her off? There had been no sightings of him since yesterday when he tried to strangle her in the emergency room. A man that large should have trouble disappearing.

There was another sound. He was opening the first door. If he went in, maybe she'd be able to run outside. She had little hope that it would work, but it was her only chance at the moment. When she heard him step into the room, she gently opened her door and watched as a man entered the room across the hall.

It was now or never.

Kate opened her door wider and flew toward the stairs. Instantly, the man shot out of the door and grabbed her, slamming her back against the wall.

Her breath was knocked from her, but only for a second. As she lifted her head, her gaze locked with his.

Her heart was lodged in her mouth as she stared up at her captor.

Gary Lloyd leered down at her. She'd never forgotten anything about his appearance. He was an extremely handsome man, one of those men who never seemed to age. His blond hair was thick and wavy and fell just below his ears. His eyes were a light blue, so pale they were almost gray. He also had the longest natural lashes she'd ever seen.

And that smile, that bright glint of even teeth that looked so sincere and sympathetic. It was all an act. He was a man without a conscience.

His eyes widened. The grin on his face sent a shudder down her spine.

"Well, well. Katie Bontrager all grown up."

When he lifted a hand to touch her face, the part of her that had frozen came to life. With a scream of rage, she lifted her hand and rammed it up into his handsome face. She didn't have a gun, but she knew how to fight.

Gary was unprepared to face a woman who knew how to defend herself. With a cry as the heel of her hand hit his nose, he backed up and tripped, falling down the stairs.

The front door crashed open, bouncing back against the wall, and Lieutenant Greer charged in, followed closely by Abram. With a cry, she flew down the steps and flung herself into Abram's arms. He held her as she sobbed out her relief and her fear. When his arms tightened, she could feel that he was shaking. She allowed herself a minute or two in his arms before backing away and wiping her eyes.

"I'm okay. Honestly. Just shaken up, mostly. Where's Marshal Delacure?"

"I'm right here." The marshal marched through the door, her gaze stormy as she took in the man moaning on the floor. "This isn't Evan Stiles. Any idea who he is? I didn't get a good look at him earlier, but I'm assuming he's the one who ambushed me. He hit me from behind."

"Yeah, I know him," Kate grated out. "I would know that face anywhere. His name's Gary Lloyd."

Abram was instantly at her side again. She knew he'd seen Gary and recognized him. When he took hold of her hand in silent support, she held tight, grateful for his steady presence to help her focus. She took a deep breath. Did she want to do what she needed to do? Once she started, there was no going back.

Lieutenant Greer stalked over to him and pulled him up from the ground, ignoring Gary's bloody nose. "Where is Beth Zook?"

Wow. Who knew the lieutenant could growl so fiercely?

"Read him his rights, Greer." Marshal Delacure crossed her arms over her chest. She was fuming. "We'll have plenty of time to ask questions at the station. I want to make sure this is done by the book."

With a visible effort, the lawman started to read the man his rights.

"One moment, Lieutenant Greer." Kate held her voice steady. She was a cop. But she had also been a victim. Never again.

Sucking in a fortifying breath, she released Abram's hand, immediately wanting to grab it again. He was such a solid man. But she was strong enough to do this. Before she could change her mind, she moved over and stood toe to toe with the man who had been responsible for so much misery.

"I want to add another charge." She watched the sneer that had risen to Gary's face alter subtly, saw the fear enter his eyes. "I want to add the charge of assault against a minor."

The room went quiet. She hadn't named herself the victim, but the weighted silence told her most of them knew she had been the victim.

"When did this happen?" Lieutenant Greer asked, his narrowed eyes never leaving Gary's face.

"Ten years ago, September thirteenth. The victim was a sixteen-year-old Amish girl. Her parents wouldn't allow her to press charges. The Amish don't often involve the *Englisch* police. However, as she is an adult now, and as this crime has no statute of limitations, I would like to press charges now. I will be available at your convenience to come in and make a statement."

No one said anything as she changed from referring to herself in the third person to first person.

Lieutenant Greer's expression didn't change, but his eyes glinted. He read Gary his rights, snapping the handcuffs into place before he led the man out the door. He gave her a sharp nod before they departed.

She walked to the door and watched as her tormentor was shoved into a police car. She'd done it. After all these years, she'd stood up to him and made him face the consequences of his actions. It was surreal, watching it play out now.

"He'll go away for a long time." Marshal Delacure laid a hand on her shoulder. "Your charge will make the case against him stronger. I think he'll spend the rest of his life in prison."

She nodded, unable to speak for a moment. When she heard the car drive away, she remembered the envelope she'd found. Removing it from her apron, she showed it to the marshal. As the woman read the contents, exhaustion swamped Kate. With a sigh, she leaned her head against Abram's shoulder. He shifted his position, putting his arm around her to tuck her close to his side. She dropped her lids for a moment, blocking out everything but him.

He gave her a gentle one-armed hug. "Hey. I'm proud of you."

She tilted her head to see his face. "Yeah?"

"*Ja.* It took guts to accuse Gary. You've been carrying that secret for a long time. I'm glad that you were able to bring it to the light."

"Adele won't have to worry about him now."

"Or anyone else." He kissed her forehead. She didn't have the energy to remind herself that they were only friends. Later.

A sharp exclamation from Marshal Delacure told her the marshal had read the part about Beth going to Lieutenant Greer. She heard the marshal's teeth snap shut with a click. Raising her head, Kate watched as the marshal snatched her phone from her pocket and hit a few buttons.

Kate found herself too tired to worry about it now and closed her eyes again, although she listened.

"Tim? Yeah. You are not going to believe this. I think that Lieutenant Greer has been keeping information from us…Obstruction, at the very least…We caught another suspect, I'm going to ask to be there for the interview…Fine, meet you at the station."

When she hung up, she stalked over to Kate. "I

know you heard me. I can give you guys a ride to Abram's house."

Kate was already shaking her head. She wasn't going to miss this. "No. Abram needs to bring his buggy home. I want to go to the station. I want to see his face when you talk to him. And—" she narrowed her eyes "—I need to formally make a statement against Gary tonight."

The marshal's gaze softened. "Are you afraid you might lose your nerve?"

Kate shook her head. Without thinking, she linked her fingers with Abram's, allowing his touch to keep her grounded. "No. I just need to be done with this. I have spent too many years carrying this baggage around inside me. It's poisoned me. I need to let it out and be done with it."

Abram squeezed her hand. "Can you wait twenty more minutes and follow me home? I'd like to be with you."

"Abram," Marshal Delacure began, a chiding edge in her tone.

"I'd like him there," Kate interrupted. "Please? Gary's actions changed the course of his life, as well as mine."

The marshal bounced her gaze between them. Her glance dropped to their clasped hands. Understanding bloomed on her face.

"Fine. Let's put this to rest."

TWELVE

Abram put his mare and buggy away as quickly as he could without skimping. "You did *gut* today, girl." He brushed the mare down. She'd worked hard and deserved a rest. "You got me there in time to help Katie. That was the important thing."

After he was done, he made his way into the *haus*. He needed to inform his *mamm* and *daed* where he would be going. There was no need for them to worry about him. He found them sitting with Sam in the front room. It was getting dark outside. *Daed* had already lit the kerosene lamps in the *haus*.

"You were able to help, ain't so?" His *daed*'s voice was as calm as still waters. Abram never knew if his *daed* was disturbed by his voice alone. He hadn't heard him raise his voice in years. Not since the last time he had argued with Levi. The next day, Levi had left. David Burkholder had never said so, but Abram knew his *daed* regretted his harsh attitude ever since. It was a testament to how much that he had never repeated that mistake. Abram and Sam had both benefitted from it.

Levi and his *daed* had long since made their amends and were very close now. He knew his *daed* and *mamm* were both thrilled that Levi had come home and was a deacon. He'd settled down and was raising a family.

All the things they had hinted they wanted for Abram and Sam.

It would have to be Sam. Linda had rejected Abram for not being able to give her his whole heart. She had been correct. Abram had been in denial. He would never be able to give any woman his heart. Any woman other than Katie. She had captured his heart years ago. Even though he'd felt betrayed when she left, he'd never let her go. While he'd only been with her a few days, the same connection that once flowed between them had bloomed to life again and deepened.

Abram didn't delude himself. He was well aware that in a few days she'd be returning to Wallmer Grove. Her life was there. He prayed she'd be able to finally find some peace and forgive her parents. And herself.

Would she forget him?

He doubted it. Just like he'd never forget her. No woman would ever be able to take her place. It wouldn't be fair to ask another woman to be his *frau* when he couldn't give her his whole self.

His *daed* was waiting for Abram to answer. "*Ja.* We found Katie. Someone had attacked the marshal and Katie, but the police arrived in time and the man is under arrest. I'm going with them while Katie makes her statement."

David and Fanny exchanged concerned glances. "My *sohn*, are you sure about this?"

He'd known his parents wouldn't like the idea. "I need to do this, *Daed.* There are things you don't know, and I can't tell you. Katie needs me there."

His *mamm* frowned. "She's not Amish anymore, Abram."

"*Ja*, I know this. But I love her. I always have. I will support her."

Sam spoke up, to his surprise. "You can't marry her. Or would you become *Englisch*?"

There was no censorship in his brother's question. Only concern and curiosity. Was it his imagination, or was there regret in Sam's voice? He couldn't think why there would be, so he focused on answering the question. "*Nee*. I will not leave the Amish church. *Gott* is first. *Gott* is always first."

His *mamm* sighed. "*Gott* be with you, *sohn*."

There was nothing more he could say. Katie was waiting with Marshal Delacure in the car. As he opened the door, he heard the marshal talking on her phone, canceling an appointment. He hopped into the back seat, wishing Katie weren't sitting up front. He had no idea how long she'd be in Sutter Springs and he wanted to spend as much time as possible with her.

A small voice in his mind chastised him. She wasn't here for him—she was here to find a missing woman and help end the drug trafficking, and maybe worse crimes. She'd already accomplished capturing a predator and would be responsible for putting him in prison, probably for the rest of his life, if Marshal Delacure was correct.

He was proud of her courage. It had taken a lot for her to step forward as she had.

At the police station, the three of them made their way inside, without speaking. Katie ended up walking between Abram and the marshal. Every few feet, her arm would brush his. He could have moved away.

In fact, he had done so once already. When she still brushed his arm, he realized she'd moved with him.

He smiled slightly, glancing down at her demurely *kapped* head. He doubted that she'd done it on purpose. Katie wasn't one to flirt or draw attention to herself. *Nee*, she was relying on him subconsciously. It pleased him, though he knew it shouldn't. He was failing miserably at keeping his distance.

The marshal stepped up to the registration window and informed the clerk that they were there to see Lieutenant Greer. Abram didn't know what had been in the envelope Katie had handed her to read. They'd had no opportunity to discuss it alone yet. Given the marshal's hard voice and the anger he sensed simmering below the surface of Katie, it had to have been something shocking.

After a five-minute wait, the trio was led into a conference room. "The lieutenant will be with you in a minute," the clerk told them.

"Fine," the marshal bit out.

A minute later, the door opened again, and Marshal Hendrix entered. Abram's eyes widened. He shot a look in Katie's direction. Her face had lost all expression. Which wasn't a good sign.

"There might be drama coming." She nodded her head toward Marshal Hendrix. Marshal Delacure strode over to him, anger vibrating in every step.

The marshals separated and stood in the opposite corner, whispering amongst themselves. He caught the words *lies* and *obstruction*. Raising his eyebrows at Katie, he said quietly, "What happened?"

She was watching the two people on the other side of the room. "I found something Beth had left in one of the rooms. Actually, she'd hidden it pretty well, so I think she knew she was in danger. What I don't know is how Lieutenant Greer is involved."

What? His jaw dropped open. He never would have suspected the police lieutenant of anything underhanded. The man was as by the book as they came.

He wanted to ask for more details. The door creaked open before he could do so.

"Looks like we have a party," Lieutenant Greer joked, wariness in every line of his face. He knew something was up, Abram figured. Why else would they have needed both marshals to come in?

"Not a party," Katie said. "I want to make my statement. I would prefer not to have to wait for the morning to do it."

"Of course," he said, nodding. "We can do that."

He looked at Abram. "I'm assuming he's here for moral support."

She hesitated, then nodded.

Abram was surprised she wasn't confronting him. But then he understood. Marshal Delacure was Beth's handler. She had been the one to develop a relationship with the missing woman, and if something sneaky was happening, she should be the one to address it.

Marshal Delacure stamped over to where the lieutenant was standing. He took one look at her face and folded his arms across his chest.

"Uh-oh," Katie whispered. "There's going to be a fight."

Abram's lips twitched. He murmured, *"Sich selbst verhalten."*

Katie snorted. "I always behave myself."

Marshal Delacure flung the envelope that Katie had

given her on the table. "I want to know what you're playing here. We found this at Beth's house. Details regarding drug trafficking and possible kidnapping. And a meeting with you!"

He blanched.

"You said you didn't know her," Katie said, keeping her voice gentle. "The first time I met you, you acted like you didn't know her or anything about her disappearance."

The man sighed and studied his shoes for a moment. When he lifted his gaze to them, a wry smile played around his lips. "Obviously, I lied."

Kate almost pitied the man. There was something so sad in his posture as he admitted to lying. She hardened her heart. If he had anything to do with Beth's disappearance, she'd do her best to see that he faced the consequences.

Lieutenant Greer stepped around the angry marshal facing him and moved to the table. He picked up the envelope and carried it to a chair at the head of the table. Once he sat, he proceeded to read through the contents. Every few seconds, his face softened.

Kate was coming to an amazing conclusion. She exchanged glances with Marshal Delacure and saw that the other woman's anger had drained. She'd seen it, too. When he finally spoke, his words came as no surprise to her, although both of the other men in the room appeared shocked.

Finally, he looked up. "I first met Bailey a year ago."

Marshal Hendrix's jaw dropped at the use of the witness's real name. "She broke the rules."

Greer shook his head. "Actually, no. When we met,

I had gone to the B&B because one of the guests reported a theft. Bailey was at the front desk. She was the most efficient receptionist. She explained she wasn't usually at the desk, but the girl who was supposed to work that night had had an emergency and wasn't able to make it. We talked for a few minutes. She made some comments that made me think she'd done some very non-Amish things, such as going to concerts. And not as a young girl. She didn't realize that I had picked up on the clues."

He paused and poured himself a glass of water. "I couldn't shake the feeling that I had seen her before. I was curious. I'll admit it. So, I started meeting her at her work. Or out in town. It wasn't long before I realized who she was. She might have been in Amish clothing, but her face hadn't changed. One of my deputies had some magazines on her desk, and Bailey St. Andrews was on the cover of one of them. But by that time, it didn't matter."

"You were in love," Kate guessed.

He nodded. "We were. When I told her that I knew who she was, she cried. She didn't want to leave, and she said she'd have to leave."

"She didn't leave, though." Marshal Hendrix sat on the edge of the table. "Why not?"

Greer shrugged. "I wasn't about to lose her. I told her that I'd give up my job. We could be relocated together. She resisted at first. But finally, she agreed. We would leave this town together. But then that kid overdosed, and Bailey was positive that he was the victim of foul play. She said she'd gathered some other evidence to prove it. We were planning on meeting to go over the notes. Then she disappeared."

"Why didn't you tell us?" Katie demanded. "If you knew, you could have helped us."

"I didn't know you. Not enough to trust you. I knew the moment I saw you that you weren't telling me the truth. Then the marshals showed up. But I wasn't sure what Bailey had found. My department has been searching for her. I myself have spent nearly every waking moment looking for her."

Marshal Delacure approached him. "When we find her, do you still want to disappear with her? You'd never be able to work as a cop again. And you'd lose all contact with the people here."

"I don't care. Bailey and I plan on getting married. I'll go wherever I need to go and do whatever job you want. All I care about is being with her."

Kate blinked back tears. *Who would have thought?*

Lieutenant Greer stood. "But now, we need to get Miss Bontrager's statement and we need to interview Gary. He's lawyered up, so we have to wait until his legal counsel arrives."

Within five minutes, Kate was situated with paper, a pen and a mug of tepid coffee to write out her statement. The lieutenant had allowed Abram to stay in the room, but they weren't allowed to talk. He wanted no chance of any details that weren't directly from her memory to appear on the paper. Any inconsistencies would be torn to shreds in court and Gary the Shark would walk out a free man.

That was not going to happen.

It took her twenty-three minutes and a half a dozen tissues to get the statement down on paper. Abram had squirmed while she sobbed and sniffled through the retelling. He wasn't uncomfortable. She saw his face.

He ached for her. It was a priceless gift. It also made her sad. She recalled the way that Lieutenant Greer was ready to ditch his career for Beth. Abram wasn't likely to ditch his faith. It was a part of him.

Could she—

No. She'd left the Amish long ago. Going back wasn't an option. It wasn't just that she was a cop. She was slowly learning to trust God again, but her faith was not nearly to the level that his was. It would be unrealistic for her to think she could become Amish and live that life without the faith it required. It wasn't an easy life. She knew. She'd lived it for sixteen years.

It hadn't seemed like too much then, but her faith hadn't been destroyed yet.

Was it destroyed, though? Granted, she hadn't communicated with God for a long time. She had gone her own way, but maybe some kernel of her faith had survived. That kernel was slowly coming back to life now.

For that, she'd be forever grateful. It would help her make it through her life without Abram. She ached at the thought of leaving him behind. But there was really nothing else she could do. Abram deserved a wife who was as strong in her faith as he was.

No, she was making the right decision. She would try to find fulfillment as a single woman. No man had taken his place before; she didn't see that changing in the near future.

When her statement was done, she capped her pen and handed the signed statement to Lieutenant Greer.

"Have you interviewed Gary yet?"

He shook his head. "No, unfortunately. His lawyer won't be able to arrive until tomorrow. So we'll have to wait. Sorry about that."

She shrugged. "Not much you can do about it. We'll have to come back tomorrow. Then we'll be able to move on."

"Oh, by the way, I thought you should know that your friend was released from the hospital."

"What!" She gaped at him.

"Yep. He's at the Plain and Simple. He's still under care, but he insisted he didn't need to remain there."

She could believe that. Shane hated hospitals, although she knew he'd take care of himself. She couldn't wait to see him!

Marshal Delacure drove Katie and Abram back to his family's home. Abram seemed to sense that Kate wasn't in the mood to talk. She felt like she'd been wrung out until she was ready to break. When they arrived back at his parents' house, they sat down and ate some of the dinner that Fanny had left for them.

Abram asked her if she wanted to sit on the front porch for a few minutes. The desire to say yes was so great that she bit her lip to keep it in. She needed to start distancing herself. The events of the night had shown her how vulnerable she was. Even worse than that, though, she was dragging Abram into her drama with her. He should have the opportunity to meet someone and marry. She was holding him back. It hurt to think of him with another woman, having children and growing old with her.

But how could she deny him that? Abram was a good and honorable man. He deserved more than she was able to give him.

With that thought, she declined to sit and talk with him. Instead, she went upstairs, her steps heavy as if her boots were filled with cement. Climbing into her bed, she let the tears streak down her face and soak into the pillow.

She'd return home free from Gary, but her heart would stay behind with Abram.

THIRTEEN

Katie slept in well past the normal breakfast time the next day. She woke when the sun was high in the sky. Her sleep had been disturbed the night before with nightmares. Most of them were too murky to recall anything more than Gary's face, although she had seen Evan Stiles's face in a couple. She woke up every hour and a half or so, then it took her at least thirty minutes to fall back to sleep.

She might have been tempted to leave her bed, but she didn't want to wander around someone else's home. When she fell back into an exhausted sleep around five o'clock in the morning, she didn't wake again until after seven thirty. Abram, Sam and David would have already left for work.

She suddenly remembered what Lieutenant Greer had said. Shane was awake, had been released from the hospital and had checked into the bed-and-breakfast.

Gasping, she threw back the covers and dashed out of bed to get dressed. Throwing her hair up in a bun, she pinned it in place before donning her *kapp*, never thinking about how natural the actions were. She paused. She'd put her hair up in that fashion daily as a teenager. When she left the community, she'd wanted nothing more to do with anything Amish. Fortunately, she'd met Holly Blake while working at the Amish-run bakery in town. Holly was already nineteen and a college student. She was looking for a roommate. Kate had moved in and found a job as a waitress. Holly was a political science major. She and Kate would talk about law enforcement. Kate realized she could help others the way she hadn't been able to help herself. The day she was accepted into a program, she felt free and empowered. She'd immediately gotten her hair chopped off to right below her ears. The first day, she felt sophisticated. Soon, she realized how much more challenging it was to deal with short hair. Ensuring it looked neat and tidy was an ongoing struggle. It would have been easier to keep it long. Then she could have pinned her hair up whenever she felt like she needed it out of the way.

She had considered getting her ears pierced—the ultimate defiance. Hair grew back in time. Putting a hole into one's ears was a bit more permanent. In the end, she decided she wasn't one to volunteer for pain that wasn't necessary.

"Boots, boots, where are my boots?" Muttering, she found her boots and tucked her feet into them before moving downstairs. Abram was in the kitchen, sitting at the table with his *mamm*.

She could do nothing to stop the surge of joy that shot through her and warmed her face.

"Abram! You didn't go to work today?" She'd hoped he might stay home, but hadn't thought it likely. He had other responsibilities.

"Clearly." He took a deep swallow of his water and

then put the cup down, smacking his lips in an exaggerated fashion. "*Mamm*, as always, your breakfast was delicious."

His *mamm* laughed. "Flatterer. Katie, there's plenty left. Help yourself."

She didn't even try to demur. Flying to the stove, she shoveled a spoonful of the sausage and egg casserole onto a plate and hurried to the table. "I remember your casserole. It still is one of the best things I've ever eaten."

Fanny blushed at the praise and smiled.

"What are your plans today?"

Kate looked at Abram. "I want to stop by the bed-and-breakfast and see Shane."

"*Ja*. I figured you would. I'll hitch up the buggy and we'll be able to go. How long do you need?"

She shrugged. "Ten minutes?"

It wouldn't take hardly any time at all to finish her breakfast and brush her teeth. On top of being hungry, she was in such a hurry to see her partner and friend, she barely tasted the food as she scooped it into her mouth, chewed and washed it down with a fresh cup of coffee.

The coffee, she had to admit, was better than anything she'd ever had at the police department.

In just under ten minutes, she was out the door and climbing up into the buggy beside Abram.

"I have so much to update Shane on."

He nodded.

She was a little startled that he didn't seem to have more to say. "Abram? Is something wrong?"

He shook his head, then shrugged. Which wasn't much of an answer.

"I'm not sure I know what that means. Yes, there is something wrong or no, there isn't? If you don't have time to take me to the bed-and-breakfast, I'm sure I can find another ride." She tried to hide the spurt of hurt she felt at his attitude.

"*Nee.* I don't mind taking you. Of course, I don't!" Abram stared ahead as he maneuvered the mare around the corner. "It's not that there's something wrong. Not exactly. I don't want you to think I'm mad or anything."

She tapped the toe of her boot on the floor as she waited for his response. "Well, then what is it?" Suddenly, she was concerned. "Did I do something wrong?"

He laughed. "Of course not! I'm so happy to get to know you again, even though I'll admit to being a bit annoyed at first." His jaw worked. "The problem is your partner."

"Shane?" Nothing could have astonished her more. "What's the matter with Shane?"

"Nothing!" He tightened his shoulders and let them drop again. "Nothing is wrong with Shane. I'm grateful *Gott* gave you someone to watch over you all these years. He and his wife sound like *wunderbar*, *gut* people."

"They are. Shane has been a big brother to me for so long."

He laughed again, but it was almost a bitter sound. "I'm being irrational. I find that I'm jealous of Shane."

"Jealous!"

"*Ja.* He got to see you grow into yourself, be more confident. There are so many memories he has that I will never share. It's not logical. I have no explanation for how I feel."

She shook her head, amazed. "I never thought of any of that. But, Abram, you know that this attraction between us, you know nothing can come of it."

His face sobered. *Ack.* So much sadness there! She dropped her eyes so she wouldn't have to see it.

"I know it. I've known it since you showed up. You aren't Amish, and I will never leave where *Gott* has placed me."

It was only a few words, but those few words took all the joy she'd felt when she'd first seen him this morning and chucked it out. The casserole she'd devoured sat heavy in her stomach.

Her heart was as gray as the thunderclouds hovering angrily in the sky above them.

Shane Pearson greeted them both like long-lost friends, despite the fact that he'd never seen Abram before. Abram liked that the man was concerned for Katie, but still respected her ability as a police officer. He found that in spite of his initial jealousy, Shane was the type of man he'd be happy to call a friend.

Katie smiled and injected a bubbly tone into her voice, but Abram was able to see through it to the shock as she saw how badly Shane had been hurt. Underneath the shock, though, her love for the man was clear. That was all Shane saw.

It had been as he'd told Katie. He had nothing personal against the man. It was the fact that Shane had been with Katie as she was growing that he resented.

Well, *resent* was a strong word. He didn't wish to deny Shane a part in those experiences. Rather, he wished he could have been a part of them, too. That might have been enough to cure him of the aching sadness enveloping his heart.

Katie took her time to update Shane on what had occurred while he had been in the hospital recuperating. She did gloss over the events with Gary. Oh, she let him know that Gary had ambushed them, and that he was arrested. She also made mention of the fact that she was pressing charges against him for something he'd done years ago.

Katie had not gone into any further details, though. Shane had stared at her, his eyes searching as though he were trying to discover her secrets, but then he let the matter go.

How much did the man know? Probably not much, Abram decided. Katie was not one to unburden herself on others. Even those who were closest to her.

"Well, with Gary out of the way, it seems to me this Evan dude is the next guy we should be looking at. Are you sure he's not the leader?" Shane took a sip of the Mountain Dew he was drinking that morning.

Abram shuddered. "How can you drink that stuff?"

Shane smirked. "Guess it's an acquired taste."

Abram was glad he'd never acquired it. "I tasted that stuff exactly once. Way too sweet for me. And I couldn't sleep that entire night. No one warned me about the caffeine level."

"The caffeine is the best part. How do you think I managed to complete all my paperwork?"

Katie laughed and shook her head at the both of them. Abram could tell by the whimsical look at her expression that she was pleased they were getting along so well.

"All right. You two are ridiculous. I just want to put

that out there, so we are all aware." Katie tugged on her bonnet straps. "To answer your question, I am fairly certain that there's someone else above Evan. Someone giving the orders. When he tried to abduct me from the hospital, he told me his boss was displeased with him."

Shane stroked his chin. "You know, by my count that makes at least twice he's botched an attempt to kidnap or kill you. And if he was the one to cut the bridle, three times. If I was any kind of boss, I'd fire someone who couldn't do the job right."

"Four times," Katie corrected him. "He shot at me when I was at Bishop Hershberger's house."

Shane straightened. "I hadn't heard about that one, kid."

She flushed. Abram liked the way the other man looked after her. When she went back, she wouldn't be on her own.

He wished he could claim that privilege of caring for her.

"Four times," Shane breathed. "Kid, I don't think he's going to be around much longer."

They all let that sink in, troubled.

"You think the boss will probably eliminate him." Katie's voice was flat.

"I do." Shane rubbed his hands on his knees, the corners of his mouth dropping down. "Actually, I'd be astonished if you found that guy alive. In my book, I'm guessing he's already messed up way too many times."

Katie sat back, unhappiness etched across her face. "So we're looking for a body."

Shane nodded. "Yep. You're looking for a body."

FOURTEEN

They sat with Shane for a few more minutes. When Kate glanced up at the clock, she gasped and shot to her feet. She had no idea it had gotten so late.

"Shane, I'm supposed to be at the police department today. They're going to interview Gary. I hate to rush."

Shane waved her apology away. "No worries. Gotta do what ya gotta do. I'm glad y'all stopped by. I have to get ready myself. I want to begin interviewing the staff today."

She gave him a quick hug, mindful of his injuries, then she was off.

"Hold on, Katie."

Impatient, she frowned as she spun to face Abram strolling toward her as if he had all day.

"What?"

"I have the keys, as they say."

It took her about two seconds before she burst into laughter at his way of saying he was the one driving the buggy.

"I wouldn't have left without you. But now that we think Evan is probably dead, as well, I'm anxious to get this case solved." The moment the words were out of her mouth, she wanted to call them back. Not the bit about wanting to find justice, but the fact that once the case was solved, she'd be gone. They both knew there was no way around that. Neither one of them was ready to admit how strong the feelings were growing between them.

It would be useless, anyway. Nothing either of them could say would change the fact that regardless of the faith that was brewing in her soul, she was not and would not become Amish. That part of her life was done.

As tempting as it might be to ask Abram to come with her when she left, she wouldn't do that. Number one, he would refuse. She knew that he was a man who put his faith first. Always. And she respected him enough that she would never try to get him to change that. She almost thought that if Abram left the Amish community, then part of his soul would shrivel.

She would never ever ask that of him.

They boarded the buggy again. Abram grabbed the reins. Suddenly, he flicked a glance toward Kate. "How would you like to drive?"

Her mouth dropped open. "You already lost one buggy because of me. Now you're just asking for trouble."

He smiled. The corners of his mouth trembled before he chuckled. She crossed her arms over her chest. There certainly hadn't been anything humorous in her comment.

"You used to always tell me I was trouble when we were growing up, remember? Anyway, it was not your fault that the buggy was destroyed. But I am serious. If you wanted to try to steer the reins, I'll let you. Here."

He scooted over slightly and handed her the reins. He stayed close in case she needed help. It was a surprisingly intimate experience. Her cheeks heated up, and she had to clear her throat several times. When his fingers brushed hers, she wondered if it was deliberate.

After about five minutes, she handed the reins back to him. She'd had all she could take. Any more and she'd melt into a puddle of goo on the floor of the buggy. She needed to keep her head on straight.

Abram didn't comment when she scooted away, widening the gap between them.

In fact, he didn't say anything until they were on the way to the police station. Glancing under her lashes at him, she saw his face was flushed, too. That hadn't been the brightest thing they'd ever done.

When they arrived at the station, they were ushered into a room where they could see the interview in progress. She hadn't known how much she needed to see Gary admitting to his crimes. While she cringed, and her stomach wanted to revolt listening to his smarmy comments and self-satisfied smirk, knowing that he was in that room, on his way to prison, because of her was a good feeling.

Abram moved closer and nudged her with his shoulder. "You okay?" he mouthed.

She smiled. Yeah, she was fine.

Or she would be.

They were leaving when Lieutenant Greer called out to her. "Kate!"

Changing direction, she and Abram crossed the room. "Yes, sir?"

He motioned for them to come with him. Confused,

Kate and Abram looked at each with raised eyebrows, but they followed without comment.

He led them into the conference room where they'd met the night before. Was that really less than twenty-four hours ago? Gesturing for them to sit, he closed the door.

"One of the officers just called in a 10-100."

Kate stiffened. "A dead body? Who was it?"

She held her breath. She could only think of two people that he would specifically mention to her. However, if Beth had been found, there was no way he would be sitting here so calmly telling her about it. She had seen his emotion the night before. No. It had to be Evan Stiles.

He nodded to her, his face solemn. Death was never something to rejoice over, not even if it involved a criminal. Death was always serious. "I'm still waiting for the photos and a positive identification. I fully expect it to be Evan Stiles."

"Do you mind if we wait here until you get final confirmation?" She had to know if it was him.

"I rather expected that you would. This room is yours until we know anything."

It was hard waiting, the dread building up inside. It felt like she would explode from the pressure building up. At times, she got up to pace, just so she could stretch herself out to give her lungs more room to breathe.

An hour later, they had their confirmation. Evan Stiles had been murdered. Shot in the head, execution-style.

Looking at his photos, she realized with a start how young he was. "He wasn't much older than a boy."

Abram put his arm around her shoulder, silently offering comfort and strength. She needed it, too. Part of her worried how she'd get by without it once she returned home.

Abram knew seeing Evan Stiles dead had affected Katie profoundly. Abram wished there were some way he could comfort her, but sometimes it was just best to be silent.

"Where do we go now?" Katie burst out. They were back in the buggy on their way home. "Gary is in jail, Evan is dead. I have no idea where to look."

"Did you ever finish going through Beth's *haus*?"

He hated the idea of taking her back there, but surely there was something they could use.

"I think that we've gotten everything we needed from there. Seriously, I don't know where else to look. Beth kept pretty much to herself. I think with the exception of Lieutenant Greer, she wasn't close to anyone."

He nodded. She was echoing his thoughts exactly. "Do you reckon it would be of use to talk with him again?"

"Nah. He's pretty much told us everything he can. I need to find another lead. There has to be something more. Something I'm missing."

"You'll find it." He pulled into his driveway. "I have every confidence in you."

She smiled, pleased. "Thanks. It's nice to know someone believes in me. I have trouble doing that myself."

He parked the buggy in front of the *haus*. A fat drop

of water splattered on the center of the protective plastic shielding inside the buggy.

A grimace marred her pretty face. "Ugh. Rain. Again. I am really looking forward to a dry sunny day."

He chuckled. "You're in Ohio in the fall. Rain is our norm. Go inside and stay dry. I'll deal with this and be in."

He laughed outright at the speed with which she bounded from the buggy.

"Hey, I'm not going to refuse an offer like that. To be in a warm house on a miserable day? Oh, yeah."

Giving him a thumbs-up, she dashed up the stairs and disappeared inside the *haus*.

He chuckled at her antics as he coaxed the mare into the barn. A few minutes later, he entered his kitchen, hanging his hat on the hook.

Katie was sitting at the table, his *mamm* and Adele with her. All three women were ignoring fragrant *koffee* in their mugs, as they talked. It was something serious. Then he remembered.

Adele had worked at the bed-and-breakfast with Beth. Katie had wanted another lead. Looked like she may have found one. He got down a mug and poured himself a mug of *koffee*. He had a feeling he was going to be leaving the *haus* again soon.

Sitting next to Katie, he saw Adele's expression for the first time. His cousin had been crying. Her lids were red and the whites of her eyes were bloodshot. Clearly, she'd been crying a great deal.

"Adele."

She shook her head, wiping her eyes on her apron. She lifted a hand toward Katie.

"Abram, your cousin came here today because she

talked with Shane. He let slip that we were looking into Beth's disappearance."

"He also said that you were at her *haus*." Adele stopped sniffling and looked at Abram. "Abram, I liked her. She was nice and never asked nosy questions. But I knew she wasn't Amish. I didn't say anything, because I might have been wrong."

Abram nodded.

"This is as far as we got before you came in. Tell us what happened next, Adele."

"After I got done talking to Shane, I felt bad. I hadn't told him something that happened."

Katie waited. Adele continued after thirty seconds of silence. "A few days ago, I went to Beth's *haus*. To see if she'd come home. And she had."

At this, Katie and Abram both sat straight, jaws nearly hitting the table in their shock.

"She came home?" Kate questioned, her voice taut.

"*Ja*. She was gathering things she'd need. She didn't even look at the mess of her *haus*. Someone had torn it to pieces. She told me not to ask questions. She was in a hurry and didn't have time to play twenty questions. She was rushing around, desperate, like her life depended on it."

They nodded. Her life probably had depended on it.

"I heard something ring. She had a cell phone. I knew for sure she wasn't Amish then. None of us have cell phones in our homes. She didn't seem to care that I saw the phone, so I figured she was leaving us. Someone called her, and it sounded like it was a boyfriend or something. When she got off the phone, she was smiling."

Abram immediately thought of Lieutenant Greer.

He had said they'd planned to enter the witness protection program together.

"So what happened after she got off the phone with her boyfriend?" Katie's eyes narrowed as she concentrated. Her mind was processing all the information, sorting it as they talked. He didn't even need to ask to know this was how she worked.

"Someone else called. Said they had information she was needing. They gave her an address. She wrote it down and took it with her when she left."

Katie sank back against her chair, a look of defeat on her face. She'd forgotten his cousin's skill with numbers, Abram realized.

"What was the address, Adele?"

She rattled it off and Katie shot back up, reenergized. "This might be what we need."

She grappled with her apron until she found the phone the marshal had given her. Dialing, she waited, her fingers drumming on the hardwood table. "Come on, Shane. Pick up the phone."

A moment later, she groaned. "Shane, this is Kate. Give me a call, please. I might know where Beth had gone after she left here."

She tried to reach Marshal Delacure next. No response. "Doesn't anyone answer their phones?"

Abram would have smiled at her grousing if the situation weren't so deadly.

"Where is that address?" he asked her when she ended her message.

She tapped out the address in the maps app. Stopped. Then she did it again.

"I don't know if this is right, but the address is Lake Sutter."

"Why would someone meet her there?"

"That's why I'm worried, Abram. At first, I thought maybe she'd gone to meet Lieutenant Greer. But he would have told us that."

"Ja?" He tried to make sense of what she was saying.

She shook her head. "It's not ideal for a meeting. But what if the person she was meeting claimed to have the evidence she was looking for? And what if they were really planning on killing her, to stop her from looking into their business? Lake Sutter might be a good place to hide a body."

FIFTEEN

Kate tried Shane's number again, but he wasn't answering his phone. Where on earth could he be? The irony of him being at the Plain and Simple Bed and Breakfast and the lead coming to find her instead didn't escape her attention. Her stint as an undercover cop had been rather a phenomenal failure, but she tried to remain positive that today would be the day they found Beth.

She started praying that they would find her alive. She took encouragement from the fact that she had been seen alive and well a few days ago.

"Please, God, let her be alive."

"Amen." She startled as Abram, Fanny and Adele all responded to her impromptu prayer.

Abram had called for a driver for them. It had taken a full hour before one had arrived. The driver turned out to be a young woman, about twenty years old, with platinum blond hair, huge hoop earrings and a tendency to snap her gum loudly. Her name, she told them, was Trina.

Despite her appearance, Trina was a cautious driver. Her shoulders hunched as she held the steering wheel tightly at three and nine o'clock, exactly the way she'd been taught while studying for her driver's license, no doubt.

The rain was coming down so hard that Trina had to set the windshield wipers at the highest speed. Each swish sent rivulets of water streaming down the sides of the window. Trina slowed down to half the posted speed. Her mouth pulled down at the corners and her face tensed.

"Are y'all sure you want to be out at the lake on a day like this?" She leaned in, nearly touching the steering wheel with her body. "It's nasty out there. I can barely see the road."

"*Ja*, we have something to do." Abram's voice was patient, but his lips were pressed tight together. He wasn't liking this any more than Trina was.

Kate understood. The same anxiety was running beneath her skin. She hoped she was wrong. That Beth had met someone who had really been intent on giving her good news.

Her gut, however, whispered that the person Beth had gone to meet had lured her to Lake Sutter to end her interference. She wanted to be positive, but in her heart, she believed if they found anything, it would be the former socialite's body.

She dreaded calling that in and coming face-to-face with Lieutenant Greer. If they found Beth's body, the lawman would be devastated. *Please, God. Let us find her alive.* Trina's tire hit a deep puddle. The water splashed up, covering the windshield, momentarily hiding the road from sight. Kate's stomach lurched as the car began to hydroplane. It skidded to the side of the road, the wheels going off into a ditch.

They were stuck. The car wasn't going anywhere. Trina began to cry.

Kate patted her on the shoulder. "Look, Trina. It'll be fine. Call a tow truck. When they arrive, I'll take care of it."

The girl settled down once she knew someone else would pay the bill. Funny how life worked that way. Kate wasn't going to judge her. Trina needed her car for her work. She had to have one that was reliable. Hopefully, they hadn't damaged anything when they'd gone over the edge. They'd scraped the grass and gravel with the bottom of the car pretty good.

The tow truck driver arrived twenty minutes later. He pulled the car back onto the road and took a quick look to be sure it was still sound.

Turned out, one of the wheels had been damaged. "It'll need to be towed. We can fit it in and get you on your way in a jiffy, but can't do that here."

"Could you let us pay for it and then you take Trina with you?" Kate couldn't afford to waste any more time.

"Umm, yes?" He cocked his head at them. "You planning on walking home or something?"

"Or something," she said, nodding.

When Kate charged the bill to the Wallmer Grove Police Department, his eyebrows had climbed under his shaggy bangs as he glanced over at her and Abram. It didn't take much imagination to know he was finding the appearance of two people dressed in Amish clothing and a connection to the Wallmer Grove Police Department incongruous, to say the least. It would take too much time to explain it. He would just have to deal with his curiosity.

"Seriously?" The tow truck driver looked like he

didn't know whether to laugh or scoff. In her opinion, either action would probably be valid.

"Yep." She left it there.

He grinned. Abram didn't grin, but he did send her a sly wink. He'd found the humor in the situation, as well. He sobered quickly. Remembering, as she did, the gravity of their situation. Every minute they spent not actively searching for Beth was a minute they were less likely to find her alive.

As soon as they were sure that Trina would be taken care of, Kate and Abram set out on foot toward Sutter Lake. They had at least a mile, possibly a mile and a half, before they arrived. The rain hadn't let up at all. They speed-walked, as well as they were able to in the slick conditions. There wasn't even any room for conversation. They needed to save all their breath for the journey.

By the time they reached the lake, Kate was exhausted. Walking over a mile in the horrible weather, leaning into the wind and the rain pushing against them at every step, was hard work. If they hadn't been drenched from the rain sloshing down on them, Kate was sure they'd be just as wet from sweating.

When this was over, they'd need hot showers, clean clothes and about an hour in front of the fireplace. Oh, and maybe a forty-eight-hour nap. Give or take an hour or two.

Kate heard a low rumble from beside her. She blinked up at Abram for a moment, uncomprehending. When she heard it again, her eyes widened and her brow arched in question. He shrugged, a half grin, half grimace crossing his face. His stomach was growling.

Add that to the list, she thought.

But first they had to find Beth and whoever had killed Evan Stiles. She knew in her gut it was one and the same person. But she had no idea who. Mentally, she crossed all of their suspects off her list— Gary was in jail; Evan was dead. And even Lieutenant Greer, whom she'd been suspicious of for a millisecond, turned out to be nothing more dangerous than a protective and concerned boyfriend.

When they arrived at the lake, they had to trudge through the overgrown grass around it. Kate's skirt was dirty and wet, and her legs bore the scratches of thorns and prickly plants by the time they managed to get all the way around the lake.

"How sure are we that this is the right place?" Abram frowned, squinting, at the smallish boathouse near the lake. The dock was about as simple as one could get. There were two small boats tethered to it, covered with tarps that looked about a hundred years old.

Spinning in a circle, Kate considered her options. There was no one, and nothing else, about.

"I can't promise anything," she replied, still working, dissecting their position in her mind, "but all my instincts tell me she's here. Somewhere."

She didn't say dead or alive. By the grimness of his expression, he had added that himself.

"Let's start looking."

The boathouse door wasn't locked. It creaked loudly when she pulled it open. Inside it was dark and damp. The odor of mildew and mold nearly overpowered them.

"Whew! Let's see if there's a window in this building." Taking her phone, she shone the flashlight around the interior. There was no window. Nor was there any evidence that Beth or anyone else was inside. Her heart fell.

She'd been hoping, so hard, that they'd find her.

"She's not here." The words fell like hard pebbles from her lips.

"We'll keep looking." Abram put his arm around her shoulders. "We'll not give up, Katie. No matter what. We'll find her."

"You can't promise that." She was grateful and touched by his willingness to walk this path with her, but she needed to be rational about it. "We're out of clues."

"We haven't searched everywhere yet," she added. Taking a deep breath, she plunged into the conversation she'd never wanted to have. "We need to have the lake dragged."

"Dragged?"

He knew what she meant; she saw it in his face. He just didn't want it to be true any more than she did.

"Yes. We need to get the scuba team out here to search the lake for her body."

Abram closed his eyes but nodded his acceptance.

"*Ja*. That would be logical. Even if we don't want it to be true. We need to know."

A sudden dread entered her heart. How would they tell Lieutenant Greer if she were correct?

Moving away from the boathouse, she called Marshal Delacure's cell, leaving her a message that they were at Lake Sutter and wanted to have the lake dragged. She knew the woman would immediately understand what she was getting at, but she spelled it out, just in case. Then she left a message for Shane to meet her at the lake.

Hanging up, she turned to tell Abram it was done.

He was standing still, his body poised, head tilted. He was listening for something. She copied his posture.

There. She heard it. A woman's moan.

Her blood pumped hard in her ears, excitement growing. Where was the sound coming from? She spun in each direction, trying to localize the noise. It seemed to be directly ahead, near the water.

Was Beth in the water?

Keeping her head low, she struggled to hear the noise over the wind and rain. "Beth? Beth! Where are you?"

She waited, holding her breath. A low moan answered her. Hurrying forward, she rushed to the edge of the dock, Abram dashing to her side. They knelt together. Carefully, she leaned over to look under the dock. It wasn't that high off the ground, but the rocks lining the ground sloping to the water were dangerous-looking. They were dark with the water, and some of them were jagged and sharp.

Beth wasn't anywhere.

The moan came again. She crawled to the other side of the dock. "In the boats."

Scrambling down, they slipped and skittered toward the two boats connected to the dock by thick ropes. The boats were small, no more than canoes. One of them seemed to sag into the water. As if the water was slowly leaking into it and it was sinking.

Clutching the wet tarp, which was slimy with algae, she dragged it back from the boat and gasped.

At the bottom of the boat, a woman in a blue Amish dress with a *kapp* that was no longer white lay still at the bottom of the boat. Water lapped gently around her still body, dark and deadly. Her shoulder was darkened and there was a hole in her dress. She'd been shot.

They'd found Beth.

The water was coming in from a hole near her feet. "Whoever shot her must have shot at her twice." She pointed at the water spilling in through the opening near the woman's feet. "That's where the water is coming in."

"She's not moving." Abram leaned over.

Beth's color was bad.

"Maybe not. But as of a minute ago, she was making noise. We have to get her out of there."

Kate frowned. They couldn't step into the boat. It would be too unsteady, and the water was too turbulent for that kind of movement.

"Maybe we can undo the rope and pull the boat to shore?"

"*Nee.* That would take too long. She's already been in the water awhile. I have a better idea."

"What are you doing?" she cried, alarmed, as Abram stood and moved perilously close to the edge of the dock.

Abram grinned and gave her a thumbs-up before jumping into the frigid water next to the boat.

The water was absolutely freezing. He couldn't stop himself from shivering, but he did his best to ignore his own discomfort to help the injured woman.

"Whoever shot this poor woman needs to be arrested." Katie's voice shook with fury.

"You're not wrong," he replied. He planted his feet as firmly as he could on the slippery rocks beneath the water.

Abram reached out and hoisted Beth up out of the boat and into his arms. Soaking wet, she weighed more than he had expected. For a moment, he staggered under her weight before he managed to steady himself. The boat shifted and knocked into him. He barely managed not to fall over backward into the frigid water.

Katie jumped down beside him. He frowned. He'd not intended for both of them to get wet. "Oops."

She looked at her apron. It was hanging below the water level. "Should have removed my phone first. How am I supposed to call for help?"

"You left messages for Shane and Marshal Delacure, ain't so?" he asked. She nodded. "Hopefully, they'll get the messages and head out this way."

"Is she alive?" Katie hovered by his side. Before he could respond, she reached past him and placed her fingers against the pulse point at Beth's throat. "Good, she has a pulse. But I don't like her color. We need to get her warm."

"Let's get up to the dock. Maybe there's a blanket of some kind in the boat *haus*." Abram nodded his head in the direction of the ramshackle structure on the edge of the dock. He was shivering in earnest, the wetness from Beth's clothing seeping into his own. He kept this to himself. Katie was shivering, too, her waterlogged dress slapping at her legs as she moved. The wind from the storm amplified every chill.

Slipping on the slick rocks, they made their way up the treacherous incline to the wooden dock. It was little more than a wooden bridge between the water and the dilapidated boathouse.

Beth stirred, coughing.

"It's okay, Beth." Katie patted the woman's arm before bringing her hand back to rest on his forearm. He didn't think she was aware of what she had done. "We'll get you dry and then we'll get you to the hospital to be looked at. You're going to be fine."

He shifted his burden in his arms before lifting an eyebrow at Katie. "Will she?" he mouthed. He had his doubts. She'd lost some blood when she was shot. In addition, Beth seemed to have slipped back into unconsciousness. All movement had stopped again. A vision of Katie in his arms as he'd pulled her from Lake Sutter. He shuddered. A new fear entered his mind.

"Has she stopped breathing?"

Katie responded instantly to the desperation in his voice. She leaned closer, her *kapp* bumping into his chin. He halted to give her better access. Her face leaned over Beth's, turning her cheek. He knew she was trying to feel the other woman's breath on her face. When her eyes slipped shut in concentration, his roamed over the two women. They were both too pale. He knew they weren't fragile, even if they gave that appearance. The past few days had shown him how strong and capable Katie was. And Beth had survived despite everything she'd been through. Still, he wished he could protect them from the evil that had invaded their world.

"She's breathing." Katie turned her head to meet his eyes. When she spoke, her voice was a low murmur. "I hear a little wheezing."

That couldn't be good.

When she backed away, he hefted Beth higher in his arms so she was more secure and began to move again. The wind bit at his face and hands. He ignored his discomfort. Although he didn't mention it, Katie had to be miserable. Her legs were bare below the end of her skirt. The edges of her lips were developing a blue tint.

Arriving at the boathouse, Katie ran to the door, her gait awkward and uneven, probably due to the chill, and yanked the door. It opened with a slow, yawning creak. He turned sideways so Beth's head wouldn't hit the door frame and entered the small building. It wasn't warm, but at least the wind wasn't blowing on them any longer. That was definitely a blessing.

"Do you see any blankets?"

Katie made quick work of searching the house. "Aha!"

Pulling a blanket out of the corner, she wrinkled her nose as a small mouse squeaked and ran under a pile of life jackets in the corner. The blanket had several holes where mice had chewed through it, but they weren't in a position to be picky. It was tricky work, but they managed to get Beth cuddled up inside the scratchy blanket. The odor of mildew rose to his nose.

"It smells."

Katie nodded. "I know. I don't see another option. I have no idea how long she's been in that water. Granted, the water isn't freezing, but it's cold enough. We have to get her warm."

If only they could leave. Then he remembered. She had called Shane several times. "When do you think your partner will get here?"

She bit her lip. "I don't know if he will. I had to leave a message. If he doesn't check his phone, he might not get it. I don't think I'll be able to call him again."

He let that sink in. If Shane never got the message, no one would know to check for them here. They would be stuck here. Unless they walked.

"We should start walking," she said, echoing his thoughts.

"*Ja.* Maybe Shane will *cumme.* If not, I hope someone will see us and decide to take pity on us."

She grimaced. "If our appearance doesn't scare them off."

"We are a bedraggled bunch, ain't so? But we look harmless enough."

Her glance held a world of sarcasm, but she contained whatever comment she might have made after peering at Beth again. It was hard to know how much the other woman was aware of or if she was able to hear them talking. He made a mental note to keep any negative thoughts to himself—at least until Beth was out of danger.

"We should grab another blanket." Katie reached out to grab another blanket, halting when a suspicious rattle came from the corner. Straightening slowly, they looked into the dark damp corner. Ohio didn't have many venomous snakes. In fact, there were only three species in the area, but one of them, a massasauga rattlesnake, was staring in their direction, its head pulled back and its rattle raised in a clear warning. Its writhing gray body was covered with round black splotches.

They were not going to be grabbing any more blankets.

"I think we should leave," he murmured out of the side of his mouth, keeping his voice low.

"Agreed. Let's go slow, though. We don't want to appear threatening." Katie moved back toward the door, her hand waving behind her as she felt around for the door. He kept his eyes on the snake so he could shout a warning if necessary. After a minute, the snake seemed to settle back down, although its malevolent gaze tracked them.

"Yes!" Katie whispered. He chanced a glance her way. She'd found the door. She pushed it open, cringing back from the wind sweeping into the room, eliminating what little warmth had been present. He preceded her through the door, bending his head against the blast of cold air. His eyes watered. Blinking, he lifted his head.

"Katie, someone's coming."

Katie emerged from the boathouse and turned to watch the person advance, squinting against the midday glare. The stiffness drained from her posture as she recognized the person moving purposefully toward them.

"Oh!" Relief shivered in her voice. "I think it's Natasha, the woman from the scuba team. I wonder if she was sent out to search for us. Marshal Delacure must have gotten my message. Well, we don't need to drag the lake, but she might have a phone. Or at least a warm vehicle."

"Why isn't anyone else with her?"

She cocked her head and watched the other woman approach. "I don't know. Maybe they're driving separately?"

The end of her sentence ended in a question. She stopped walking, her face growing tense. Kate no longer seemed excited to see the scuba diver.

Unease slithered down his spine. Something wasn't right. Her stride was almost angry. If there weren't a dangerous predator inside the boathouse, he would have suggested they return there rather than face the menace he saw in Natasha's posture.

"If we start now, maybe we can go around the other side and go the long way to the road."

But they'd be too slow.

"Too late for that, Abram." Natasha reached them. Her dark eyes took in the whole scene. She sneered at Beth's still body in his arms. "That woman has caused me more trouble than she's worth."

Katie shifted. Natasha pivoted to face her, drawing a revolver from the back waistband of her pants. She held it like she knew what to do with it. Her expression said she had no problem with murdering three people.

They had run out of options.

SIXTEEN

Abram didn't know what sort of gun or what caliber it was. All he knew was that it looked deadly and Natasha had it aimed right at Katie. "Don't even think about it. I know exactly why you're here. You gave me a scare when I found the gun in your apron. I'm not going to give you a chance to make my life any more difficult. I have everything the way I like it, thank you very much."

Abram processed what he was seeing and hearing.

Natasha Booth, respected daughter of Sutter Springs's mayor and a member of the scuba team, was the leader of the crime ring that had forced Beth into hiding. More than that—this woman was a cold-blooded killer. She had killed Evan Stiles. And, even though it hadn't been said yet, she was the one who'd shot Beth.

By the way she was talking, she had no intention of letting any of them leave, alive.

"Natasha, what's going on?"

Abram couldn't believe Katie's casual tone. She looked relaxed, but he knew her well enough to know that she was poised to act. Was she stalling for time?

It made sense. If she bought them enough time, maybe Shane would show up. Or perhaps if she kept Natasha talking long enough, she'd figure out a way past her or be able to subdue her.

He looked between the two women. Natasha was taller and muscular. But Katie was strong and intelligent. She was also fierce, and he knew that she never backed down in a fight.

Natasha took a step closer. "I knew when Evan saw you at Beth's house you were not what you seemed. The idea you might have been a cop crossed my mind."

"The explosion—"

Natasha shook her head. "I told Evan it wouldn't work. He insisted Beth would come back. A bomb would silence her for good. Except you and your partner were the ones who got caught in it. Not that I minded."

"You killed Evan." Katie's voice hardened. She wasn't asking a question.

"Of course, I did. He'd messed up too many times. People were bound to recognize him sooner or later." She smiled. It was almost painful, the loveliness of her smile in the face of such horror. She had no regret for any of the pain she'd caused.

"Ishmael?" he rasped, recalling the youth who'd overdosed. The *Englisch* police had written it off as an accident, but the teen had denied it.

She shrugged. "He wasn't supposed to be harmed. It should have been simple. But when people don't follow the rules, they get hurt."

"He refused to sell drugs to other schoolchildren," Katie hissed, fury in every line of her body. "You poisoned him, didn't you? And Beth found out about it."

Natasha's hold on her gun tightened. Abram expected a bullet to explode out of it at any second. She waved the gun briefly at Beth before training it back on Katie. "She was going to ruin everything. The previous boss had made mistakes, and when he went down, I saw an opportunity."

"You're the mayor's daughter." Abram shook his head.

Natasha's upper lip curled. "Fat lotta good that's done me. All my life, I've been restricted to act and look a certain way. My friends were picked based on suitability. Well, I found the chance to do something more and I took it. I was not going to allow some goody-goody destroy what I had built by running to the police. She actually thought she'd be able to run from me."

A dark light entered her eyes. She was done talking. Abram's breathing was constricted. How would he save Katie? She began to bring the gun around.

She was going to shoot Beth.

Abram swung away, protecting Beth with his back. At the same instant, Katie went into motion, jumping forward and stretching out her arms for the gun. Natasha fell backward. With a holler, she rolled to her feet.

"Get her to safety!" Katie kept her eyes trained on the furious woman slowly regaining her feet, the gun in her hand aimed straight at her.

Katie's glance flashed briefly in his direction before returning to Natasha. In that instant, he knew she was torn between fighting Natasha and protecting the civilians. He had to remove himself from that equation.

His heart pounded in his chest. Every fiber of his being urged him to place himself between Katie and

Natasha, but he knew she wouldn't want that. Katie was doing her job now, and she would expect him to do his part to help her.

Where could he take Beth? He couldn't go into the boathouse, not while it was infested with poisonous snakes. He stepped off the main part of the dock and flattened himself against the side of the boathouse. There was a very narrow strip between where he stood and the dock ended. If he breathed too hard, they'd go over the edge. His arms were beginning to ache with holding Beth, but there was no place to put her down to give them a rest.

"I've got her!" he yelled to Katie, letting her know he'd take care of Beth so she could deal with the dangerous villain.

Kate kicked the gun from Natasha's hands. It flew through the air and landed in the water with a solid *plop*!

The woman yelped, then immediately snarled. Her hands curved into claws as she shifted closer and closer to Kate. Keeping her gaze firmly locked with Natasha's, Kate danced away from her, every movement a deliberate taunt. She needed to keep Natasha's focus on her so she wouldn't go after Abram and Beth.

Abram could take care of himself, but she knew he'd die to save Beth.

No one would die today, if she could help it. Not Abram or Beth. Not even Natasha, assuming it was possible to take her down easy. Hopefully, Shane got her message and help was on the way.

She needed to keep the angry scuba diver busy until the authorities arrived.

Natasha was out of patience. She shouted and charged, her head lowered as she leaned forward.

Abandoning her thoughts, Kate met her charge and shoved. Natasha stumbled back. She tripped over the pile of lumber lying by a corner of the boathouse. Grabbing a long board with jagged ends, she advanced on Kate again. A confident smile spread across her face as she glanced at the board.

Kate followed her eyes. Four nails with wicked, sharp rusty points jutted from the end. She'd have to be careful. If only she had some sort of shield. Backing away, she scanned the area.

"Katie!" Abram kicked a long wooden oar her way. Natasha went for the oar, but it skidded past her. Angrily, she swung her board at him. He jerked away, shielding Beth, but the edge caught him. He hissed as a nail struck him. When he went over the dock with Beth, Kate nearly dropped the oar. She held on to it at the last instant. She needed to take care of Natasha first.

She heard some splashing in the water, and a low soothing whisper. It was hoarse, threaded with pain. She knew that voice. Abram was alive. He was hurt, but he was conscious and aware.

Natasha and Kate circled each other like boxers in the ring. Natasha was strong and fit, and she was taller than Kate by a good four inches. She also had the advantage of a dangerous weapon in her hands.

Kate, however, was a Wallmer Grove police officer, trained in self-defense. She knew by the heavy way Natasha moved about, and the awkwardness of her stance, that while the paramedic took good care of herself, she had no real training or fighting experience.

Would that be enough to give Kate the edge she

needed? It had to be. She couldn't wait for Shane to show up with the cavalry. She needed to end this so she could go check on Abram and Beth.

Resolve settled over her like a cloak. When Natasha swung at her with the board, Kate ducked under the wood and jammed the blunt end of the oar into the other woman's stomach.

"Oof." Natasha dropped the board, her arms instinctively moving in to protect her belly.

Kate ran at her, and wrapped the bigger woman up in her arms like a child. Natasha struggled against her hold, but Kate had her arms pinned against her sides. She swept her leg under Natasha's and they both fell to the dock. With the speed and efficiency born of much practice, Kate had her on her stomach in under five seconds with her wrists crossed behind her.

"Abram!" Kate shouted, her eyes scanning wildly. She had nothing to contain Natasha with and was forced to sit on her back to hold her down.

Grunting, Abram emerged over the side, Beth over his shoulder. His arm was at an odd angle. He must have broken it when they went over.

Gently, he settled Beth down. His gaze scanned Kate for a few tense moments. Finally, he smiled and moved into the boathouse, limping. She frowned. What else had he injured? He returned, carrying a long thick cord and handed it to her.

"Danke," she murmured, using the Amish word for *thank you* without a thought. Biting her lip, she transferred her focus to tying Natasha up good and tight. She had no future here with Abram, and she needed to make sure he knew that. The last thing she wanted was to hurt him again. Even though she knew they'd

already gone too far for that. She would hurt both of them when she left.

This time for good.

A distant siren caught her attention.

"Ah," Abram murmured, "I think Shane's coming to rescue us."

She snickered at his wry comment. A moan sobered her. Beth was waking.

"Watch her."

Abram nodded and stepped closer to Natasha, earning himself a string of insults from the paramedic. Knowing he'd keep an eye on the woman, Kate flew to Beth's side.

"Beth? Can you hear me?"

Beth's mouth worked. Kate frowned, not liking the ashen cast to her skin.

"Feel sick. Stomach."

Beth started to gag. Kate swiftly worked to help her move to the edge of the dock. She wished there was a way to get her warm. Beth had lost quite a bit of blood. She wasn't out of danger yet.

When the sounds of retching faded, Beth had a little more color in her cheeks. "Who are you?" she croaked, opening her eyes and blinking at Kate. They were a startling clear green in her pale face.

"My names Kate Bontrager," Kate said, smiling. "I'm with the Wallmer Grove Police Department. My partner and I were sent here to find you."

Beth pushed herself up to a sitting position. "I remember you. You were there…"

Kate nodded as Beth let the statement die. Regardless of the circumstances, she was still in the witness protection program. The rules about not discussing the past were drilled into witnesses. If they broke the rules, they'd be kicked out of the program. She nodded to show she understood.

"We've apprehended the leader of the drug-trafficking ring, the woman who shot you. She'll be going to jail. And her accomplices, Evan and Gary, have both been dealt with, as well." Now was not the time to go into how Natasha had killed one of her own men. Beth just needed assurance that she was now safe and that those who had tried to do her harm were not going to come after her again. She felt for the woman, having had to hide twice.

"I didn't think she'd find me. But she did." Beth closed her eyes. "I would do it all over again, you know. Those kids, they needed someone to take their side."

"You did that, Beth. You should be proud of yourself."

Kate stood as two police cruisers rolled into view, lights flashing and sirens screaming. The sirens cut out abruptly, although the lights continued flashing, splashing blue and white on the water.

Shane stepped out of the first car. The doors to the second cruiser opened. She recognized Marshal Delacure, who was with another police officer. Beth gasped as her handler came into view. Delacure knelt beside Beth and they began whispering together. Kate moved away to give them some privacy.

Lieutenant Greer jumped out of the police cruiser and dashed over the soggy ground. Beth sat up, tears in her eyes. He joined her and the marshal. Marshal Delacure was talking rapidly, probably explaining the process of witness protection and the risks.

They probably wouldn't listen, anyway.

Shane strode to Kate. "How ya doing, kid?"

She shrugged, afraid that if she opened her mouth, all her emotions would spill out for everyone to see. She was holding herself together by a thread.

He slung an arm around her shoulder for a quick squeeze, then released her. "Glad we got here in time. I'm always ready to ride to the rescue."

Abram joined them with a snort. "*Ja*. What would we have done without you?"

She had to laugh. "Okay, guys. Yes, Shane. We're glad you're here for the cleanup." She yawned. "I'm done. I need to sleep for a week."

"After you write your report."

Groaning, she nodded, rubbing her eyes. "After that."

An ambulance pulled in behind the two police cruisers. The doors opened and two paramedics hopped down. Their eyes bulged and jaws dropped as the police officer walked past them with Natasha. Kate's makeshift handcuffs had been replaced with genuine ones. The officer nodded once at the stunned paramedics before placing her hand on Natasha's head and stuffing her neatly into the cruiser.

The somber pair of paramedics approached and checked out Kate, Abram and Beth. Beth was loaded into the ambulance. Marshal Delacure conversed with the paramedics briefly before climbing into the back with Beth.

"That arm looks painful," a paramedic commented to Abram.

Kate bit her lip, concerned. She hated to think of Abram in pain. It galled her that he had gotten involved in this messy world of crime.

He smiled, but his jaw was clenched. He was in pain but wouldn't admit it. Men.

"I think you busted it," Kate told him bluntly.

He winced. "*Ja.* When I went over the dock, I used my arm to protect Beth and landed on it. I also twisted my ankle. That's why it took me so long to get back to you. I needed to get her safely up. It wasn't easy."

She stared at him. "Not easy? You carried a full-grown woman up a wet embankment with a broken arm and a twisted ankle. Abram, that's amazing."

He flushed at her praise.

Shane strolled over to them. "I need the car," Kate said to him. "Any chance you can hitch a ride with the officer before she takes off?"

He pulled the key from his pocket and tossed it to her. "Sure. I'll see you later."

He jogged up the hill, catching the officer before she backed up and left. Only a true friend would have given in to her request without questions. She turned to Abram.

"Come on." She waved for him to accompany her. "I'm driving you to the hospital myself. There's only one ambulance."

"*Gut.*" He fell in line beside her. "I think we should talk."

It was the last thing she wanted to do, but it had to happen. Now was better than waiting. Like pulling a Band-Aid off fast. It hurt, but sometimes doing it slowly or hesitating hurt more.

She let him get in and helped with the seat belt, knowing he'd struggle with only one hand.

"I'll try not to hit any bumps." She slid behind the

wheel and started the car. The cruiser pulled smoothly off the grass and onto the road.

A thick silence fell between them. After five minutes, she took a deep breath. Abram beat her to it.

"We've found Beth and the leader of the drug ring here in Sutter Springs has been arrested," he mused. "It's been an eventful day."

She snorted. No one made understatements like Abram. "Yeah, you could say that. A little too eventful." She gestured toward his arm.

"I don't know. We're alive. So, it's *gut*." He looked out the window. "What now? You've done everything you were supposed to do."

This was it. Her chest felt hollow, like her heart had been harvested, leaving a hole in her chest.

"Now, I go home," she whispered. Her hands clenched on the wheel. She blinked back the wetness searing her eyes. A single tear slipped out. "I go home, and life returns to normal."

He turned to face her. "It won't, ain't so? You can return to Wallmer Grove, but will it still be home? Will you miss me, Katie?"

"What kind of question is that?" she huffed.

"An honest one. I will miss you every day of my life, Katie. But I'm not sad that we met again."

"I'll miss you," she muttered, her voice nearly inaudible. "My life isn't here, though. I'm not Amish anymore."

"You could be."

Her breath stalled in her chest.

She pulled into the hospital parking lot and drove under the emergency room carport. "Abram, I left the Amish world behind almost a decade ago. That's not something I can go back to. I'm sorry. I truly am."

The tears were falling faster now. He wiped her cheek with his uninjured arm. "*Ja*. I'm sorry, too. I love you, Katie Bontrager. If you ever decide you can live the Amish life again, you know where I am. I'll be waiting for you."

She sat, frozen, as Abram released his seat belt and opened the door. Her eyes followed him as he walked through the sliding doors and out of her life.

SEVENTEEN

"Done."

Kate jabbed the send key on her report and leaned back in her desk chair. She hooked her finger through the handle of her favorite mug and took a sip of the steaming French vanilla cappuccino. She'd splurged for the first time in a month as a small reward for another successful arrest. She frowned into the mug. It used to feel good to close another case. To take one more drug dealer off the streets. She'd been meticulous in making sure the proper procedures were followed, not wanting to leave the defense attorney a millimeter of wiggle room. Kate took another small sip from her mug, breathing deeply as the sweet aroma wafted past her nose.

Even her coffee wasn't as enjoyable as it once was. Too sweet.

"Hey, kid. Sitting on your hands again?"

She snorted at the remark, mock glaring over her mug as her partner, Shane, strolled down the aisle between the desks at the Wallmer Grove Police Department, his heels clomping in a steady rhythm on the tiles. Shane, she thought fondly, was the only thing that felt the same since she'd returned.

He came closer and leaned back, half sitting on her desk. "Out with it, kid. I've kept my mouth shut for weeks."

"What?" she stalled, knowing he wouldn't be fooled or put off. He had given her space, but she knew Shane. Now that he'd decided to speak his peace, he wouldn't be moved until she gave in.

Narrowed eyes pinned her in place. "Don't give me that. You've come to work every day, smiling that big fake smile to me, trying to act like everything is peachy. Well, I'm not buying it."

Sighing, Kate leaned back in her chair. "Really."

She took a sip of coffee, mostly to occupy her hands.

"Really." He mimicked her tone. "It's that Amish dude, isn't it?"

She choked on the coffee. Using the word *dude* to describe Abram was just wrong.

Shane waited until she could breathe again. "Am I mistaken?"

He'd been patient long enough. "No, you're right, but it's complicated."

He nodded. "It always is. But I still want to know. Explain *complicated*."

"Well." She used her toe to swivel her chair from side to side. "You know that I grew up in that community. Abram, he and I were special to each other."

He nodded, his gaze sympathetic. Encouraged, she continued.

"I guess we both assumed that one day we'd get married and have a family. Until Gary." She could see the light dawning.

"I know that you pressed charges against him. It never occurred to me when we accepted this assignment that you'd run up against someone like him. I'm glad he's in prison. I'm also glad you were able to have a hand in that. I take it you knew him before he hurt you."

She grimaced. "Yeah. He worked with my father. He gave me the creeps. When I was sixteen—" she paused "—you can guess what happened."

His eyes were round with horror. "Oh. Kate, you can stop."

She couldn't. "No, it's fine. My parents were very strict. And very conscious of how others saw them. They blamed me. I couldn't take the shame and the guilt. Maybe if they'd lived, things would have improved. But they didn't. I was so alone I fled. Got out of there so fast. I never told anyone I was leaving. Not even Abram."

"He must have felt awful."

It was painful remembering how she had doubted him. He was the most honorable man she knew, and she had hurt him so bad he'd never gotten over it. Neither had she.

"He felt betrayed, and he was. I hurt him so bad, Shane."

"Kate." He leaned closer. "Does he still blame you?"

She shook her head. "No. In fact, he told me he loved me and wanted me to stay."

He had wanted her to stay, to be his wife. He might not have said all that, but she knew it. Could she have traded in her life for the Amish way, for Abram?

"So, if he forgave you and doesn't blame you anymore, why do you still blame yourself?"

Stunned, her jaw dropped. "I don't. I mean, I couldn't—" She stopped, her mind whirling. "It's not that I blame myself. Not exactly. It's more like I don't know how to move on from what happened. How do you go back to where it happened?"

"Kate, I don't want to tell you how to live your life, but I'm going to, anyway. If you have an opportunity for love and happiness, you need to ask yourself if you really want to let it go. Love is something pretty special."

She stewed on the revelation for two days before she finally made an appointment to speak with the department counselor. In the week before her appointment, she came up with twenty different reasons why she needed to cancel it. She started to dial the number several times. Each time, she halted before hitting Send.

"This is something I need to do, God. Something I need to do so I can heal and get on with my life. Give me the strength, please."

The day of her appointment arrived. She approached it with the same joy one would a root canal. To her surprise and relief, it wasn't as awful as she'd feared. Oh, it was challenging, and in some ways, it was dreadful. She swallowed her reservations, though, and made a second appointment.

It was almost Thanksgiving when she realized that her self-flagellation had stopped. She still harbored some guilt. She didn't know if she'd ever be rid of it all. But she'd let go of the ugly rage she felt against herself and her parents. Regardless of what had happened in the past, she had put Gary the Shark away and had rescued Abram's cousin from him.

Abram.

Each day, the longing in her heart grew. The business and clutter of her life became increasingly unsatisfying. She wanted more. She wanted to live a life where she worked with her hands and family was more important than the bottom line. She wanted to know that God was the first priority.

And she wanted to be a wife and a mother.

Mostly, she wanted to be Abram's wife.

I'll be waiting for you.

She sucked in a breath, holding her hand over her heart as she recalled his parting words to her. Was he still there, waiting for her?

She had no reason to doubt it. He'd never forgotten her, even after ten years. Certainly, he wouldn't forget her after such a brief separation.

Could she join the church? Yes. She was ready to make that commitment to God. And she felt no sorrow about giving up her job. She'd miss Shane, but he'd understand. He and his wife could visit.

Grabbing her laptop, Kate tapped out a quick resignation letter. She read it to make sure it sounded the way she wanted it to, then sent it to the printer.

Standing, she strode to the printer and took the letter. It was warm to the touch. With a flourish, she signed her name and headed to the captain's office. She could wait, maybe think about it more, but what would be the point? She was as sure about this as she'd ever been about anything.

She knocked softly on the door.

"It's open."

Pushing the door open, Kate stepped inside the captain's office. "Do you have a minute, Captain?"

Captain Murphy eyed her sharply. "I do, Kate. What's on your mind? Although, I think I have an idea."

Kate blinked at her superior officer. "Oh. Well, I just wanted to let you know that I am thinking of resigning from the police department."

The captain's eyebrows rose. "Thinking of resigning? Then, I can persuade you to stay?"

"That didn't come out right," Kate corrected her. "I have decided to resign. Here's my letter."

Setting the letter on the desk in front of the captain, Kate stepped back and waited, hands clasped behind her back. Now that she had done it, all her nerves had fled. She was at peace with her decision.

Captain Murphy picked up the letter and read it, her lips pursed. When she had finished, she set it down on the desk. "I'll be sorry to see you go, Kate. You're an exemplary officer. I know you have the ability to go far. If you stayed, I'm sure you'd be promoted in the near future."

"I don't desire promotions, Captain. My heart is no longer in the job."

It never had been completely, but she didn't think the captain needed to know that.

Captain Murphy sat back in her chair. "So, you're leaving us. I'm not surprised. I've sensed you haven't been satisfied since you returned from Sutter Springs. I guess I hoped you'd shake it off. I can see now that you won't. I accept your letter of resignation. Are you sure you won't change your mind?"

"No, ma'am. I'm leaving the department. I plan on returning to Sutter Springs. I have someone waiting for me there."

"Actually," a familiar dry voice said from behind her, "that someone is here."

Joy and disbelief sparked in her heart as she whirled to see the man who held her heart.

"Abram!"

She was resigning. Abram couldn't squelch the grin that had formed when he'd heard her say she was returning to him. He could have saved himself the trip, but it had been worth it to hear those words.

When Shane had seen him entering the department, a knowing smile had crossed his face. "Ah, you're here to see Kate. She's in the captain's office. I just passed there."

He pointed in the direction. Abram had felt awkward going toward the office. It wasn't in his nature to be nosy or intrusive. But Shane had seemed to believe it would be fine. As soon as he heard the gist of the conversation, he realized that Shane had wanted him to know that she was leaving her job and returning to him with no reservations.

It was a good call. He might have wondered if she'd shown up in Sutter Springs if she could truly be happy. Hearing from the captain that Kate had not been happy in Wallmer Grove went a long way in soothing the guilt that she had left a career she'd worked hard for to embrace their life.

"Abram, what are you doing here?"

Before he could answer, Captain Murphy stood and walked to the door. "Kate, I need to go check on something. Why don't you and Abram use my office for a few minutes? Plenty of privacy if you shut the door."

When she was gone, he stepped into the office and

pulled the door closed. Then he turned to answer her question. "I'm here because I'm not *gut* at waiting. I know I told you I wouldn't interfere, but I couldn't do that. I'd forgotten something." He reached out and took her hands. The arm he'd broken barely twinged anymore.

"I see your arm's better." She smiled.

A laugh built up in his chest. He restrained it, letting a chuckle break free. "*Ja*. I had a cast for a few weeks. The physical therapist gave me exercises to do at home to help me regain the strength."

That was not what he wanted to talk about. Not at this moment.

"I had to see you. I love you, Katie. I loved you when we were younger. I've always known you were the one for me. Even after you left, my heart couldn't open enough to truly love another woman. I didn't think I could love anyone. Until you came back."

She touched his cheek with her hands. "I'm sorry I hurt you."

"Hush. I understand."

"Yes, but I realized that part of me still blamed myself."

His eyes widened. "You were a young *maidel*. How could you have been to blame for any of it?"

"I know. I believed I wasn't worthy of love. Not from God and not from you. I was wrong, on both counts."

His heart twisted inside his chest, imagining her alone and scared, feeling like she couldn't even turn to *Gott* for refuge. He carefully slipped his hands from hers and encircled her. He hugged her to his chest like she was fragile and might break in his embrace. The ache inside him melted as she snuggled in closer. Resting his chin on her hair, he sighed, allowing himself to enjoy holding her close.

But only for a second. They must do this the proper way. Backing up slightly, he looked down at her. His gaze fused with hers. More of his fear vanished. Her eyes were clear and sure.

"You are worthy, Katie. So worthy. I'm sorry your *mamm* and *daed* were not supportive. None of what happened was your fault. In fact, your experience has saved others. Who knows how many others might have been hurt if you hadn't put Gary in prison? Now that he's in jail, though, any of his potential victims are safe."

She pulled away from him. Had he said something wrong? Fear constricted his breathing.

"Dear Abram." She placed her palm against his cheek. The warmth sank into him. "I love you, too. I always have. I'm sorry I ran, but I was able to leave and get the training I needed to bring him down. So, I think God was protecting me and guiding me, even while I was intent on ignoring him."

"Maybe so." He still hated to think of her hurting. "You're coming home, then?"

She nodded. "Yes, but, Abram, even though I love you, we have a long road to go before we can be together."

He knew that. Didn't much care for it, but he understood. "*Ja.* You have to join the church."

"Yep. That's my plan. I hope to meet with Bishop Hershberger as soon as it can be arranged. I know it will take a while. I'll have to meet with him several times."

"I'd say it'll be at least six months."

She winced. He knew the feeling. "Well, six months will be worth it to get to where God wants me to be. I'm done trying to do things on my own. Then we can talk about courting."

He grinned. He wasn't thinking of courting. He was already planning on asking her to be his wife when six months were over.

Six Months Later

Abram hitched up his buggy and set out toward his brother Levi's *haus*. It was a church weekend, and everyone was gathering there. He'd helped Levi, Sam and *Daed* move the furniture and set up the church benches inside the living room the day before.

Abram had never felt nervous about going to church before, but today was different. Today, Katie was joining them as a full member of the Amish church. He had every intention of asking her if he could drive her home after the service and the community meal.

He wasn't nervous that she'd say no. They'd become so close the past six months their affection as teenagers seemed weak compared to what it was now. They were more than two people in love. They were best friends and told each other everything. He'd never been one to confide his deepest thoughts to anyone but *Gott*, but Katie was the one exception.

For the rest of his life, he would hide nothing from the amazing woman *Gott* had placed in his life.

First, he had to get through the rest of the day.

When he saw her in her deep rose dress with a matching apron and a crisp prayer *kapp* covering her lovely hair, though, his heart nearly burst from his chest. What an amazing woman! If it was in *Gott*'s plan, she would soon be his wife.

The day dragged on. He laughed and spent time with his family and friends, but in every instance, he was hyperaware of where Katie was. When the meal was done, he saw his chance and took it.

Jogging to her side, he scanned the area to make sure no one could hear them. "Katie, can I drive you home?"

Flushing, she ducked her head, a smile hovering on her lips. "You may." Then she whispered to him, "About time, too."

He laughed. His Katie would always tell him exactly what she thought.

An hour later, they were on their way. Abram directed the buggy down a dirt road that had very limited traffic and pulled over to the side.

"This isn't the way to where I live," she pointed out. Her voice was prim, but her lips twitched with the effort to hold in a grin.

"I wanted to talk with you." He half turned on the bench so he could take her hand. "You're Amish now."

He winced. Not an auspicious beginning.

Her eyes widened. "So I am!"

"Stop!" He laughed. "I'm trying to propose."

Her face stilled. "What about a courtship?"

"Katie, we've known each other all our lives, with the exception of the ten years you were away. We've spent the past six months not courting, but still, I felt like we were walking out."

She nodded. "Yeah, I thought so, too."

He took a deep breath. "We are not a strictly farming community, so we have more freedom. I already spoke with the bishop. He said if you agreed to marry me, we can get married at the end of June."

"June. That's only four weeks from now." Her eyes were misty.

"*Ja*. I'm ready to begin our life together. Katie, will you marry me?"

That grin finally broke free like a rainbow after a storm. "Yes, I will marry you! As soon as it can be arranged."

Emotion stormed through him. He couldn't speak he was so overwhelmed. Instead, he took her face in his hands and pressed his lips to hers, letting the love in his kiss do his talking.

EPILOGUE

Two Years Later

Katie set her broom aside and pressed a hand to her abdomen. The pains were getting closer. She wasn't worried yet. Abram would be home in the next ten minutes. An hour ago, she'd gone across the street to their *Englisch* neighbors and asked to use the phone so she could arrange for a driver to bring her and Abram to the hospital. She'd also contacted her doctor to let her know of the baby's impending arrival.

The baby's foot pressed against her side. She massaged it. "Soon, little one. Soon. We have to wait for your daddy to come home."

She hummed as she waited. Her overnight bag was sitting on the bench inside the door. Her gaze wandered around the open kitchen, lingering on the small homey touches. A needlepoint framed on the wall from her sister-in-law, Lilah. The new cabinets Abram and Sam had made. The buffet in the corner where she kept the dishes Fanny and David had given them for their wedding.

Walking over, she picked up a plate and smiled.

Most girls picked their colors young, and they start getting their dishes to make their collection one at a time for birthdays and Christmas. That way, when they start their own home, they have what they need. Katie had had no dishes, or anything else, when she wed Abram. He hadn't minded.

All I want, Katie, is you, he'd told her.

His parents knew this. They'd surprised her with a set, one very like the set her own folks had started to present to her before they'd been killed.

The gesture, and the love and acceptance behind it, had touched her. She and Abram had found a place close enough to his family that he could still assist them and continue working with his father and brother, but at the same time, they had their privacy.

Bailey had been moved, although Katie had no idea where. That was the nature of witness protection. She suspected that the woman was still being hidden in an out-of-the-way place. Lieutenant Greer had retired and gone with Bailey. She hoped they had found the happiness that she had found with Abram.

It saddened her that she would never hear from the woman, but she was happy that Bailey was safe.

Hooves clopping on the driveway brought her out of her reverie. Abram was home. A quiver of joy jolted through her. They'd been married almost two years, but her heart still sped up when he came home to her and the life they were building together.

Abram banged through the door, his face splitting into a wide grin as he spotted her. "Katie! It's *gut* to be home."

He swept her into his arms, rubbing his nose against hers. She laughed as his beard tickled her chin. Dipping his head, his mouth brushed against hers for a sweet kiss before he stepped back.

"I missed you today. How are things here?" He touched her cheek with a gentle hand. Before resting his palm on her belly. "And how is our *boppli*?"

She grinned. "Our baby is saying he or she will be born today."

She waited.

He nodded. "That's *gut*—"

She knew the exact second his brain caught up with what she'd said. Those dark eyes widened. His face paled.

"Today? Today!" His hands flashed up to cup her face. "How are you feeling? Are you well?"

She smiled. "Relax. I'm feeling fine."

A sudden pain made her catch her breathe. She gritted her teeth as the ache spread across her lower back and into her lower abdomen. "Okay, that was the worst one so far."

The remaining color fled from his face. "We have to call for a driver. Do you know where your bag is? And—"

She clapped her hand over his mouth. Abram was always so calm. It was strange to see him so discombobulated. Practically in a panic.

"I've already called for a driver. He should be here any second. And my bag is there, by the door." Kate pointed to the bench.

Abram leaned his forehead against hers. "I'm sorry. You're taking this better than me." He looked into her eyes. "I just can't bear the thought of anything going wrong."

Oh, her sweet man. Katie's heart melted. "All will

be fine. Let's just focus on getting through the next few hours."

The driver pulled in, and within minutes, Abram and Katie were on their way to the hospital. Katie wasn't feeling so sanguine when they arrived at the hospital twenty minutes later. The contractions had increased in frequency and intensity. She grabbed Abram's hand and squeezed with each pain.

At one point, he winced. She opened her mouth to apologize. He kissed her forehead and shook his head. "Who else would you depend on at a time like this? Squeeze as hard as you need to, Katie. I can take it."

She took him at his word.

Their arrival at the hospital was met with a flurry of activity. Katie wasn't able to focus on anything but the birth of her first child.

Four hours later, Mary Frances Burkholder was born.

Abram held his breath as the nurse handed him his daughter, wrapped like a burrito in soft pink blanket. Her little face scrunched up, then relaxed in sleep. Doubtless, his *mamm* would say she looked like him or Katie. Mothers seemed to be able to point out similarities like that, though he had never been able to see it in one so small.

Mary opened her eyes and blinked up at him.

She had his Katie's eyes, a deep blue. He said as much to his wife.

The nurse behind him chuckled. "Many babies have blue eyes. They may change."

"Hmm," Abram replied, neither agreeing nor disagreeing. She could say what she wanted, but he was sure he was correct.

Katie laughed softly from the hospital bed. "If you say so. Oh, Abram, she's beautiful, isn't she?"

Looking at his wife's shining face, emotion lodged in his throat, making speech impossible. He contented himself with a nod. He carefully stepped closer to the bed and lowered himself into the chair. Mary yawned and closed her eyes.

He cleared his throat. "I can't believe she's ours."

"We're blessed," she agreed, her voice soft with affection.

Abram straightened, lifting his gaze to her. "Katie?"

"Yeah?"

"You're going to be a lot busier than before," he murmured.

"I know." She wiggled around until she was in more of a sitting position. "I was talking to your *mamm* and Lilah about that the other day. They had lots of good advice to offer."

He could tell she was serious. "Do you ever regret not remaining a police officer? Your life was so much more exciting."

"Exciting?" She frowned, tilting her head to gaze at him with those dark blue eyes. "Abram, I was living a lie. My heart was never in being a cop. I never wanted anything more than I wanted to be your wife and raise a family with you. It was, and is, my truest wish."

Smiling, he glanced down at the infant sound asleep in his arms. "Sorry. I know I'm being silly. I just had to ask. There is nothing glamorous about our life. It's very hard sometimes."

"Yes, it is. It's also an honest life, surrounded by good people who love God. I missed this life for so many years, but refused to dwell on it. Now, I'm home. Where I was always meant to be."

Careful not to wake the baby, Abram scooted to the edge of his chair and leaned toward her. She met him halfway, her lips soft against his. The kiss flooded his soul with love.

She was right.

When they were together, they were both home, where they belonged.

* * * * *

If you enjoyed this book, don't miss the other heart-stopping Amish adventures from Dana R. Lynn's Amish Country Justice series:

Available now from Love Inspired Suspense!
Find more great reads at www.LoveInspired.com.

Dear Reader,

I hope you enjoyed Abram and Kate's story. I first introduced Abram in *Amish Country Threats*. He had a small part to play, but I thought he'd make an interesting hero. A middle child, he's one who has never doubted his faith in God. It has guided him his whole life and helped him navigate any troubles. The one wound God has not yet healed is his broken heart.

Kate was only sixteen when she abandoned God, Abram and all things Amish. A case she's working on forces her back in close contact with all of the above.

I hope you were touched by her story to reclaim her faith and to fall in love with Abram all over again!

I love connecting with readers! You can find me on Instagram, Facebook and on my website at www.danarlynn.com.

Blessings,
Dana R. Lynn

WE HOPE YOU ENJOYED
THIS BOOK FROM

LOVE INSPIRED SUSPENSE
INSPIRATIONAL ROMANCE

Courage. Danger. Faith.

Find strength and determination in stories
of faith and love in the face of danger.

6 NEW BOOKS AVAILABLE EVERY MONTH!

LISHALO2021

SPECIAL EXCERPT FROM

LOVE INSPIRED SUSPENSE
INSPIRATIONAL ROMANCE

Witness Robyn Lowry doesn't remember the crime she witnessed—but someone wants her dead. Keeping Robyn alive long enough to testify is US marshal Slade Brooks's hardest mission

Read on for a sneak peek at
Hiding His Holiday Witness *by Laura Scott,*
available November 2021 from Love Inspired Suspense.

Robyn thrashed helplessly in the river current, her body numb from the twin assaults of shock and the ice-cold water.

Gasping for air, she managed to keep her head above the water for several minutes and strained to listen. She'd heard two gunshots moments before Slade had gently pushed her over the ridge, but now there was only the rushing sound of water.

Did that mean they were safe? She had no idea.

And where was Slade? She tried to turn in a circle, but the river was moving too fast for her to take more than a quick sweeping glance around to look for him.

She knew she couldn't stay in the water for much longer. With renewed determination, Robyn angled toward the shore.

Up ahead was a large tree branch hanging over the water. With herculean effort, she reached up and snagged the branch. She used every last bit of strength she possessed to pull herself up and out of the water.

Her feet found the ground, and she emerged from the river to sprawl on the grassy embankment.

"Slade!" Panic clawed up her throat, threatening to strangle her.

She didn't know who she was or who was after her. She couldn't do this alone.

"Robyn!" The sound of her name made her want to weep with relief.

A splash caught her eye, and she saw a dark shadow getting out of the water about twenty yards from where she lay.

"Robyn, I'm so glad I found you. Let's get into the cover of some brush, okay?" Slade's voice was near her ear. "We want to stay hidden from view."

Because of the gunshots.

With Slade's help, she stood, and together they moved away from the river into the wooded area.

"Are you going to start a fire?"

"Not yet. I don't want to draw undue attention if someone is out there looking for us."

"For us? Or me?"

He hesitated, then said, "I'm not leaving you alone, Robyn. We're going to stick together from here on out."

Until when? Her memory had returned? And what if it didn't?

Don't miss
Hiding His Holiday Witness *by Laura Scott,*
available November 2021 wherever
Love Inspired Suspense books and ebooks are sold.

LoveInspired.com

LOVE INSPIRED

Stories to uplift and inspire

Fall in love with Love Inspired—
inspirational and uplifting stories of faith
and hope. Find strength and comfort in
the bonds of friendship and community.
Revel in the warmth of possibility and the
promise of new beginnings.

Sign up for the Love Inspired newsletter
at **LoveInspired.com** to be the first
to find out about upcoming titles,
special promotions and exclusive content.

CONNECT WITH US AT:

f Facebook.com/LoveInspiredBooks

𝕏 Twitter.com/LoveInspiredBks

LISOCIAL2021